ELIJA

ELYON'S WARRIORS

EVE LANGLAIS

Copyright Elija © Eve Langlais

Cover Art © Covers by Julie

Produced in Canada

Published by Eve Langlais

http://www.EveLanglais.com

eBook: ISBN: 978 177 384 4381

Print ISBN: 978 177 384 4398

ALL RIGHTS RESERVED

This book is a work of fiction and the characters, events and dialogue found within the story are of the author's imagination and are not to be construed as real. Any resemblance to actual events or persons, either living or deceased, is completely coincidental.

No part of this book may be reproduced or shared in any form or by any means, electronic or mechanical, including but not limited to digital copying, file sharing, audio recording, email and printing without permission in writing from the author.

CHAPTER 1

"You actually located Atlantis?" I couldn't help but squeak as Tamara informed me they'd found the lost city, which was actually an ark sent by Heaven.

The Heaven.

And not a place in the sky as indicated by the Bible but some kind of super spaceship with a God and angels and a weird mission to seed planets so they could collect soul juice when people died. As to how we found out… Angels had recently arrived on Earth, upheaving our concepts of God, Heaven, and Hell.

Lilith, my good friend and coworker, who'd joined us for our impromptu meeting, skipped surprise and went right to the nitty-gritty. "Is the ark still capable of flight?" By ark, she didn't mean the kind that floated on water. The Atlantis was a massive space-faring living vessel. Convoluted sounding but true.

"Seems to be working," Tamara informed. "The Atlantis heaved itself out of the valley it was hiding in with no issue and, after taking care of that two-timing Jesus, took off."

"Where did it go?" I asked as I shoved up my glasses. "I thought it was supposed to evacuate people before Hell arrives." As in the actual Hell, which was like a mega spaceship—or asteroid with a propulsion system—newly arrived in our solar system. It wasn't common knowledge yet given the space agencies hadn't spotted it. Once they did, though, I expected chaos and anarchy. The news wouldn't go over well.

At my query, Tamara shrugged. "No idea where it went. Noah said something about refueling—"

"Wait, when you say Noah, are you talking about *the* Noah?" Lilith lilted the query.

"One and the same. Noah, as in the ark and the flood and all that jazz." Tamara waved her hands. "He's alive and not. My understanding, in our brief time together, is the ark absorbed him and they share a symbiotic type of relationship."

"Damn," I exhaled. "That's insanely cool."

"Terrifying too. You didn't see what the Atlantis did to Jesus Christ." Tamara's lips flattened and her expression turned grave as she explained how God's scion on Earth had betrayed them and tried to use the Atlantis to bargain for a position with Hell. The ark, which was apparently not only alive but sentient, took offense and blasted Jesus to pieces.

In other words, don't piss it off.

"Did Noah say when he and the ark would come back?" Because my greedy biologist mind would give anything to study it.

"Not an exact date, no. He did tell me to start screening people for transport, though."

"Screening them for what, exactly?" I wondered if I'd fit any criteria laid out.

"Basically, looking for a mixture of young and old, of good character. No violent sorts, and he said something about weeding out the covetous since they tend to cause trouble."

"That's pretty vague," I opined.

Tamara rolled her shoulders. "I'm aware, and the fact we can take a very limited number is going to cause trouble."

"Not to mention, how are the governments going to react?" Lilith, who used to be the communication director at Novae, a company invested in getting humans into space, zeroed in on a big problem.

Me, the person who dealt in biology, added another. "What about the ratio of races? I assume we'll want to ensure we get a sampling from every ethnicity."

To which Tamara sighed and said, "Which

might be difficult given the ideology of many will outright reject anything the angels say. There will be accusations of false gods and even people who will welcome an invasion from Hell."

"Because people can be dumb." It was true. I'd seen it my entire life. Just like people could be mean. I'd been born to immigrant parents, and despite the fact I spoke impeccable English, people often resorted to looking at my exterior to make judgments. It didn't help that my name, Cindy-lu fit into their ill-conceived Asian stereotypes. Then add in the fact I wore glasses, was petite, had high grades, and participated in clubs that my peers at the time called geeky, by the time I graduated at sixteen with honors, I'd heard every rude name in the book plus a few extras.

"It's our job to root out those who can't get along," Tamara stated. "The only good news about our task is Zakai says most physical ailments won't be a concern, as the ark can handle minor issues. Additionally, once the reinforcements from Heaven arrive with a new Jesus Christ, he can give them God's blessing of health."

It still blew me away to know Jesus Christ was a job of sorts, and not an actual person. Actually, the way it had been explained to me, Jesus Christ was essentially God's clone, just a less powerful version.

"Are you sure we want another Jesus Christ,

given the last one turned out to be a turd?" Lilith didn't sugarcoat it.

"We can only hope he was an anomaly. Can you imagine how epic it would be to have a true healer aboard with the refuges?"

Lilith's brows rose. "Actually, that's not something we should advertise. Can you imagine the mobbing by the desperate if it were known miracle-level healing was available?"

My nose scrunched. "Lilith is right. This has the potential to get ugly really quick. We'll have to make sure when the Atlantis returns that its location is hidden and well-guarded."

"I'll make sure to reiterate that to Zakai, but back to our first problem. How do we start the screening process?"

Being a bit of a jokester, I suggested, "We could post ads on social media."

Lilith pursed her lips. "Because an ad saying 'looking for people who want to colonize another planet before Hell wipes out Earth' won't cause a panic."

"We don't need to mention the Hell part, do we?" Tamara gnawed her lower lip. "We could keep it more generic and say something along the lines of 'looking for people for an isolation experiment to test for long periods of space flight.'"

"Make them think it's a simulator instead of reality." I nodded. "That's actually not a bad idea."

"It won't be long before scientists realize the thing they think is a giant asteroid headed for the sun is actually being guided to Earth," Lilith pointed out.

"Which leads us back to another problem; notifying Earth's leaders so they can help in the effort. While the ark and even the ships we've been working on will save some, if word gets out we need to evacuate, it will give other space agencies time to maybe successfully launch flights of their own."

"We have less than nine months." Lilith reminded us of the tight timeline. "And that's just for the Hell ship. Aziel says they'll send scouts first." Aziel being her angelic boyfriend. She'd been the first to make contact with the angels.

Me, I'd now been hanging with them for a few weeks in an underground bunker. I still missed my cat, but it was better knowing my baby was being spoiled by my neighbor than the fear that had gripped me when I'd been imprisoned with no idea when I'd get back to care for her.

At least the angels had provided ample distraction. I still hadn't gotten over my awe at their wings and the fact they could fly. I'd even mustered up the nerve to ask one of them if I could study his form. Elija, a grim angel who rarely smiled, had uttered a flat, "No."

But I'd not given up.

I drummed my fingers on the table in the room

we'd taken over for our impromptu meeting. Just the three of us for the moment. The angels tended to confer together and do their own thing. As for the rest of the people—aka humans—in the bunker, we wanted to hold off telling them about the Atlantis, because if Jesus Christ could be turned to the dark side, then chances were, we had at least a few potentials in our own group that would betray.

"I'm going to devise some tests to try and weed out those who think with their fists and show selfish traits. Lilith, can you figure out how to get people to apply without causing panic?" Tamara offered a task to Lilith, leaving me wondering what I could do to help.

"What about me?" I asked.

"You're in charge of flora. We need as many varieties of seeds as possible. A new planet might lack the proper nutrition, so we'll also want fauna as well from every type. Fish, birds, mammals, reptiles."

I frowned. "Given we'll need more than a single mating pair, that will take much room."

Tamara's lips curved. "Actually, according to Zakai, we don't need the creatures themselves, just the eggs and sperm to make them."

I couldn't help but blurt out, "Are they going to do the same thing with humans?" Would no one actually be saved, just their genetics?

Tamara's lips turned down. "While the ark will take some people, to ensure species continuity, yes, there will be some harvesting of us as well. It's the only way to ensure we have a big enough genetic sampling to thrive. Keep in mind, in a world that numbers billions, only thousands of the currently living can be saved."

A sobering reminder. What chance did I have of making it?

We broke up our meeting with a promise to keep things quiet as long as we could.

My mind whirled with the many things that had to be done. Getting seeds sounded all well and good except for the fact I wouldn't find what I needed at a local store. A full variety meant I'd need access to the seed vaults located around the world. Heavily secured places, which would require a ton of paperwork to access, and likely a solid negative reply if I asked to take samples. I didn't have that kind of time.

Hence why the moment I saw the grim Elija stalking through the halls, I planted myself in his path and chirped, "Just the angel I needed."

"Do you require assistance?"

I nodded. "I need your help breaking into a secure location to steal some seeds."

CHAPTER 2

THE HUMAN FEMALE BLINKED AT HIM FROM BEHIND HER thick-rimmed glasses and waited for a reply.

An easy one. "Stealing is against God's laws," he stated.

Did that send her scurrying in shame to pray for forgiveness?

Nope. She pursed her full pink lips before saying, "What if I said we needed those seeds because it's an emergency?"

"Why not ask for them?"

"Because then I'd have to explain to some very skeptical sorts that Hell is coming to demolish Earth, which would lead to me being laughed at because no one would believe me, and insisting will most likely have me thrown into a hospital for a mental health evaluation."

He frowned. "Why would they scoff at the truth?"

"The truth as we know it. But in case you haven't noticed yet, humans aren't always easily persuaded. Or have you forgotten how long it took Aziel to convince Lilith he wasn't a fake angel?"

"This is different. Soon, all on your planet will be able to see Hell's approach."

"But they won't believe it's Hell," she insisted. "They'll assume it's some new asteroid."

"If they won't believe the truth, then they'll die."

"According to you. What makes you think anyone outside our group will believe you?"

His feathers ruffled. "Elyon's warriors do not lie."

"They'll accuse you of lying about that too. Then there's the horrible types who'll want to bargain with Hell."

"Hell doesn't bargain. It takes."

"Again, they won't take your word for it, especially once they realize the evacuation plan is only going to take a fraction of the population. But that's not my current dilemma. While Tamara and Lilith hatch a plan to find suitable colonists for the ark, my task is acquiring a wide variety of flora and fauna for the voyage and eventual colonization. Given the flora is easiest, I figured I'd start with that task first, meaning I need to gather unmodified seeds. We're talking no GMO, no splicing, but original strains.

Some of which are extinct now on Earth due to certain farming and pesticide measures. Lucky for us, most seeds can be found in secured vaults around the world. The problem being I can't just walk in and walk out with what we need."

"I will not steal." Elija took the commandments seriously even if his demeanor was more light-hearted than his companions. He'd disobeyed once before, and it didn't end well. He never made that mistake again.

She sighed. "Well, that's disappointing. Guess I'll have to find someone else to help me."

"You are going to continue with this plan?" He'd assumed saying no would end it.

"What part of 'we need those seeds' did you not grasp?" She huffed. "Don't worry yourself about it. I'll handle it." She stalked off, petite and pert in her snug trousers and shirt.

Determined, too. He'd been observing her since his arrival at this hidden facility, what the humans called "an abandoned military research and development base." For some reason, she drew his eye more often than other humans, and he couldn't understand why.

Yes, she was attractive. Possibly intelligent, even if he couldn't always tell given how quickly she spoke and went off on subjects of which he knew very little. A warrior had no need to know how things grew. Nor where his food came from.

Until recently, he fed exclusively on ambrosian, a substance produced by their cantorii, the living vessel they used to travel the galaxies. He'd since tried human fare and, to his surprise, enjoyed the many flavors and textures. The humans had elevated the consumption for bodily health to a level he'd never expected. And Cindy-lu wanted to ensure that they brought that variety of consumables when they left for a new planet to colonize.

A commendable task, but he still wouldn't abet her in theft.

A device at his waist pinged. A human contraption called a walkie, which they'd been using while planet-side since they didn't dare use their HALOs. Short for Heaven's Astral Linguistic Ordinance, they were part of God's blessing to all his angels that provided communication as one of its functions. As to why they weren't using it? The HALOs when activated were a shining bright beacon to the demons on Earth. Seeing as how they were doing their best to keep this place hidden, they couldn't activate them for fear of drawing attention.

He pulled the walkie from his hip and depressed a button. "Elija here."

"Find me in the weapons training room at once," ordered Metatron, his principality and the one in charge of the angels on this mission.

"Is there a problem?"

"Possibly. I'll explain to you and the others once you're here." Metatron ended the communication.

Elija quickly headed in the opposite direction of Cindy-lu, his rapid stride ensuring people moved out of his way. The tunnels might be tall and wide enough for winged angels, but many of the humans were leery of getting too close. His glower probably didn't help.

The training room he entered offered the size needed for them to practice their skills. Lofty enough they could use their wings to do leaps and swoops, a padded flooring for the times they fell hard or got knocked down. It also provided privacy once they secured the door. No one would be able to listen in.

Upon his entrance, Elija noted Metatron on the far side of the room, quietly conferring with Zakai, recently returned from a successful mission, where they located the ark previously sent to shepherd the flock left behind on Eden. AKA guide the humans off the planet they renamed Earth.

Aziel was also present, sparring with Munna and Eoch at the same time. A testament to his skill. Then again, Elija could do the same. It was why he and Aziel, along with Leox—who stood back, observing the practice—had been promoted to archangels. They'd proven their skill at battle. At least Elija was back in fighting form. Not too long ago, his wing had been shorn in a demon skirmish. Thankfully, Jesus Christ had repaired it before the scion turned traitor.

Missing were Jir and Huud, most likely aboard the cantorii keeping watch on the approaching Hell behemoth. He'd checked on it during a stint in the Echo chamber. Eyed it and noted, while sections of it appeared to have expanded since their last known sighting, other parts had vanished. Blasted, or excised. Hell found it easier to get rid of rather than fix severely broken parts.

Or could it be someone actually managed to damage it?

Elija couldn't have said where the strange idea came from. Heaven's fighters certainly didn't have the capacity to do true damage to it. God wouldn't let them fight with mechanical weapons. They used melee weapons and learned to wage combat with their bodies, which left them vulnerable in space. The cantorii had no means of attack. The only thing of note they carried that could have been used to go on the offense, Heaven's flame—a beam of intense heat that eradicated all in its path—couldn't be used in war.

God's rule. Cleanse an offensive building or area on a planet, yes, but use it against Hell's squadrons or the massive moving legion itself? Forbidden.

Sometimes, when having a particularly bad day, he'd wonder, why? Because the rule cost angelic lives. How many cantorii had been blown to pieces by the faster-moving Hell scout and cruiser ships armed with deadly weapons?

If only they could have fought, they might have saved some cantorii and their crew. But they always turned and fled. The humans didn't have that option, though. Only a fraction would escape this rock. The young. The wise. The fertile that could parent.

Once the rest realized they'd be left to face Hell, how would they react? Judging by the way war had been perfected over the centuries of history he'd perused, it would be violent. The humans would use weapons of such devasting damage they might very well destroy themselves trying to render Hell impotent.

Given Metatron's recent secrecy and many absences, he had to wonder if the ancient angel—who once accidentally alluded to his age in a speech—had thought about Elija's suggestion of mustering the humans to counter Hell's invasion. At the very least, it might slow down Hell's armada and prevent them from destroying the fleeing colony ships and the Atlantis.

Metatron noticed his arrival and offered a slight head nod before murmuring, "Let us begin."

"Should we say a prayer?" Leox asked as they gathered in a loose circle that included the principality.

For a moment, Elija would have sworn Metatron

wanted to say no; instead, he offered a very pleasant, "An excellent idea. Will you lead us, Leox?"

The angel knelt, wings splaying behind him, the ultimate supplicant position. With a rustling, the others shifted their weight before ultimately joining him.

Leox began. "Our Father who art upon Heaven, hallowed is thy name. To your flock we have come, to deliver your word and to deal with those who trespass against Elyon. On this day, we ask your blessing as we guide this lost and floundering flock into the light that will feed the kingdom come, Earth giving its life to Heaven. Amen."

A chorus of amens followed and the slither and ruffle as they rose to their feet.

Metatron began without pleasantries. "As you all know, Hell has exited the spiral arm for this galaxy and is approaching the planet."

"At its current pace, we have nine Earth months before its arrival," Zakai reminded, as if they didn't already know.

"It doesn't provide much time to evacuate anyone," Aziel added, looking as grim as ever. The only time his angelic brother smiled was around his mate, a human named Lilith, the pairing ironic given how much they disliked each other at first.

"I'm aware of the short window of opportunity to save some of the flock. At least there is a positive. The Atlantis appears fully functional."

"Has it returned?" Elija asked sharply. He'd not heard any news since it dropped Zakai and disappeared.

"No," Metatron replied, "but the Atlantis has been in contact with Tamara and has informed her that it will require a few days of astrayla collection before it returns."

That brought a frown and a query from Elija. "Why is the Atlantis speaking with a human instead of you?"

Metatron shrugged. "I don't know. But Zakai has a theory."

All eyes went to the slim angel who'd come out of his self-imposed exile on board the cantorii to help the humans. Although Elija had a sense this change had more to do with Tamara than an obligation to the flock on Earth.

"The Atlantis, and its principality, Noah, had a difference of opinion with Elyon. It appears they were commanded to wipe Eden and start over with a freshly grown flock. However, rather than obey, Noah had the Atlantis cut off communication with Heaven and allowed the humans to continue as they were." Zakai spoke with more confidence than Elija recalled him having since his return from his abusive imprisonment in Dante's Inferno.

"They disobeyed God," Leox pointed out in shock.

He wasn't alone. Elija had learned his lesson when it came to not obeying orders.

"The choir and their ark disobeyed what they felt was an unjust order lacking in compassion for the innocent. They spent a long time waiting for Elyon's retribution. When it didn't come, they went into hibernation. When Tamara found the baetylus" —an element of the ark that allowed keyed-in holders of it to find its location—"she woke the Atlantis. It saw Jesus's perfidy, which only reinforced their distrust of Heaven, hence why they have chosen Tamara as their conduit for communication." Zakai spread his hands. "While not ideal, it is better than the alternative." An allusion to the fact they would have had one less ark to re-establish the flock elsewhere.

"How many can the Atlantis take?" Aziel asked.

"No idea." Zakai shrugged. "An exact number hasn't been given. What I do know is we haven't much time to make a selection. The Atlantis wants to be gone before Hell's scouts arrive."

That raised Elija's brows. "Given how fast their scout ships can move, that could be any day now."

"Which the cantorii is watching for." Metatron paused. "We also have the Russian government and military involved. They have been briefed on the situation—"

Elija interrupted. "Aren't the Russians the

enemy of Americans?" The country they were currently using as their base.

"Yes, but the NATO countries believe it's just a giant asteroid heading toward the sun, and they're prepared to handle this without our help. They refuse to discuss nuclear tactics with us."

A reply that had Aziel snorting. "Because they're convinced we're not who we say we are. Lilith and I tried speaking with a highly-ranked commander who accused us of working for their enemy. Much like my first encounter with Lilith, General Bellwether assumed my wings were artificially created and that we were, in his words, 'fucking with him.'"

"What can these Russians do to help?" Aziel queried next.

Elija actually knew the answer to that since he and Metatron had discussed it. "They have missiles that might be capable of taking out Hell's scout ships once they reach Earth's atmosphere."

"That's rather close," Zakai noted.

Metatron spread his hands. "It is closer than we like, but we don't have much other choice. Their space craft aren't well equipped for combat. I've got Eoch working with them to improve their current design in a time frame that doesn't make them useless."

"We should be using Heaven's flame to blast them," Aziel muttered.

Leox gasped. "God says the holy fire is only for the burning of heretics."

"Doesn't that describe Hell's minions?" Aziel countered.

Elija, for all his devoutness, agreed with Aziel.

"We are not here to discuss the theology and reasoning behind God's decree. What I would like to talk about is what we can do to convince other countries that Hell presents a real threat so they'll agree to join the space defense endeavor. If they would listen and cooperate, they could ready a space fleet that could ravage the enemy."

"You think the humans can prevail against Hell's forces?" Elija couldn't help his skepticism. He'd never seen anyone other than Heaven manage to strike a serious blow. Even then, they only managed to damage and slow the behemoth.

Always fleeing. Never managing to do real damage because God would order them to retreat.

"Don't underestimate them," Metatron advised as he held up a device the humans called a tablet. On it, he brought up images and flicked through them. Ranks of soldiers marching, massive moving armored vehicles blasting, flying craft shooting at each other. "Eden's flock is quite innovative and stubborn. Many will want to fight. The question will be if their technology can stand against the might of Hell."

"And how many will turn to the dark side," Munna's ominous addition.

"A fair amount I would guess." Metatron stated it bluntly. The war images disappeared and the tablet screen turned black.

"What of the Iscariot?" Zakai asked about the ark Heaven sent. "Do we know how many it can take and how long before it arrives?"

"It should have been here by now," Aziel noted.

"But hasn't been detected," Zakai interjected. Then added, "It could be they're cloaked to avoid detection, but they could have uncloaked long enough to contact us and make us aware they've arrived to the galaxy."

A somber Metatron stated, "The Iscariot is no longer coming."

That led to some stirring and Elija stating, "What do you mean not coming? It was expected to arrive well before Hell." Heaven sent it the moment they'd found Eden and realized it contained a lost flock—and a treasure trove of suul.

Metatron met their gaze solidly as he announced, "Elyon ordered it home."

"Why?" Elija blurted out.

"To ensure it didn't fall into Hell's hands."

"But what about rescuing the flock?" Aziel exhorted.

Zakai answered for their principality. "Our God

doesn't care about the flock. He's more worried about losing an ark."

"It makes sense." Leox jumped in to defend Heaven's decision. "After all, we found the Atlantis. There's no need to risk two arks."

"Actually, Heaven doesn't know about our finding the ancient ark," Metatron's quiet admission. "And the recall of our choir isn't the only command from Elyon. He ordered that we deposit everything we've collected from planet Eden, including humans, back onto the surface and to direct Heaven's flame onto the nearby moon."

It took Zakai only a second to understand what this would do. "If we destroy the moon, it will kill everything on the surface of the planet."

"You must have misunderstood. There's no reason why we shouldn't save what we can." Elija couldn't hide his shock.

Leox bowed his head. "His will be my command."

"Are you addled?" an angry Zakai spat. "That command is wrong. Elyon is angry the humans aren't groveling in worship. So he's going to ensure they are punished for their temerity while, at the same time, ensuring there's nothing left for Hell to collect."

Rather than deny the claim, Metatron nodded, leaving Elija conflicted. Ever since the incident, he'd unwaveringly obeyed God's command. Yet listening to his angel brothers, it appeared not all of them agreed with Elyon's dictates. It shocked to know Metatron, the person who spoke with God, had lied by omission about the discovery of the Atlantis.

Leox once more differed in opinion. "Who are we to question God? As Elyon's Warriors, it is our duty to obey."

Aziel cast him a sharp look. "I won't obey an order that will murder billions."

"Me neither," Zakai huffed.

As for Metatron, his lips pinched. "Thou shall not murder is a commandment."

A reminder that left Leox struggling for a reply. "But that doesn't apply to Elyon's Warriors. We are the stanchions of justice, the defenders of Heaven."

"We are not murderers of the innocent, though," spat Aziel. "How can you even consider obeying after having spent time with the humans? They do not deserve annihilation."

On that, Elija actually agreed.

Leox remained steadfast. "If we fail to obey his command, he will judge us with his holy might."

"I'd rather die with principles than live as a coward with regret," Metatron quietly stated.

"I shan't abet."

"I won't force you to do anything against Heaven or God. But I also won't allow you to impede our efforts to evacuate this planet. You are to return to the cantorii for a contemplation period in solitude."

Leox fisted his hands by his side. "That's not necessary. I would never work against you."

Metatron stared at him.

Leox left, his wings tense.

After his departure, Metatron eyed them each in turn. "Anyone else want to be absolved of duty?"

Elija contemplated it, given Metatron's decision put him at odds with his own morality. Obey God or follow his brothers and save the flock?

"God usually has his reasons," he murmured. "Perhaps we simply can't see it yet."

"Perhaps. Well, that concludes this meeting. Elija, why don't you take a turn aboard the cantorii." Metatron made it sound like a suggestion.

Elija recognized the punishment. He could no longer be trusted because of his beliefs.

Because he followed God.

"At once, Principality." A stiff acceptance followed by silence as he exited. No one stopped or followed because they weren't done discussing their plans to save the planet. A planet God wanted destroyed.

As Elija stalked past the humans scurrying about busily, he found himself wondering about Elyon's plan.

And his role in it.

CHAPTER 3

I didn't take Elija's rejection to heart.

Much.

It did kind of sting that he accused me of theft. I didn't see it as stealing the seeds but as ensuring they actually served a purpose rather than be destroyed. My intentions were honorable.

But I still needed help. Hence why I went hunting for the big boss of the angels. Metatron, which sounded like a Transformer name. The man himself could have been a robot with his rigid expression, all hard planes, and alpha attitude. Yet, despite his stern demeanor, he didn't seem like a bad dude. I'd had a few conversations with him, mostly him asking how my work was going—I'd been developing a hydroponics system for human-made spaceships that would hopefully sustain the passengers on board for a long voyage.

He understood the importance of my work and might hopefully offer a solution—AKA volunteer one of his angels—to help me with my task.

I found Metatron exiting the training room and striding for the cafeteria, a popular place with everyone, given the cooks kept making us the most delicious treats. I'd never been more shocked than when I found out angels only drank some stuff called Ambrosian, which Tamara, who'd tasted it, declared bland. *"I'd rather eat peas,"* she'd stated, her most hated vegetable.

"Excuse me, sir," I chirped as I quick-walked to reach his winged back. "If I could speak with you a moment."

Metatron didn't blow me off. He whirled and asked, "Is there an issue?"

"No, and yes." I jumped hastily into my explanation. "It has to do with the Atlantis. The supplying of it to be exact. My assigned task is to gather seedlings for the journey, as many varieties as I can, which, given the size of this world, would involve an insane amount of travelling and time. Time of which we have little. Then there's the actual issue of where we get the samples. Regular stores and nurseries can provide some of what we require, but their offerings might not be of the best quality. But"—I took a breath before launching again—"I could get better quality specimens inside some specific seed vaults."

He beetled his brows. "What is a seed vault?"

"They're secure and tightly climate-controlled vaults around the globe. Many countries have created disaster-proof storage areas for the seeds of all the species of fauna that grow in their area. Including untainted, original strains, before GMOs and hybrids."

"And we need to collect from each of them?" I nodded, and he then queried, "How many?"

"More than we could visit before Hell arrives. But there is a better solution. A place that takes duplicates from around the world and keeps them locked away. The Svalbard Global Seed Vault is a supersized and totally protected location. Visitors are not allowed inside, and it's guarded with modern tech."

"You may tell them of the emergency to convince them to donate it."

My lips pinched. "We've been reaching out. It's not going well." I'd contacted some colleagues in my field, people I'd worked adjacently with for years. The problem with telling them that the recently spotted giant asteroid was actually Hell on a course to wipe out Earth? The mockery landed swift and fierce, and with today's ability to communicate, word spread and I quickly got the nickname Doomsday Cindy. This, in turn, led to even more people refusing to talk to me or the others involved.

I put it to the angel boss bluntly. "Convincing them would be easier if you actually showed yourself and let some of the people we're dealing with see you exist."

His lips pursed. "Last time we tried, Aziel got taken prisoner."

Someone else might have winced, but I could say with all honesty, "He wouldn't have come to harm. We just wanted to study him and see if he told the truth and that his wings were real and not mechanical attachments."

"He's not a liar," Metatron offered indignantly.

I lifted and dropped my shoulders. "According to you. All we saw was a big angry dude, wielding a sword, with giant smoky-colored wings. According to our Bibles, that should have made him evil."

"Wing color has nothing to do with morality."

I rolled my eyes. "I know that now. But then, we had a lot of questions, and if we introduce you to the world, people will want to be convinced you're real and not an elaborate hoax."

"No. I will not pander or play games because humans can't grasp the truth when they hear and see it."

"In that case, I suggest we tackle the seed problem by simply taking them."

"Go ahead." He didn't question my suggestion.

"I'm going to need help getting past security and

then removing the seeds to somewhere that can accommodate them before the voyage on the Atlantis. I tried asking Elija if he could help me retrieve the seeds but he, um..." I hesitated before blurting out, "He refused on account we would be kind of stealing them. I tried to explain how we don't really have a choice, but—"

"No need to say more," Metatron interrupted. "Elija takes Elyon's commandments quite literally. He's young and has yet to understand that sometimes rules must be broken. In this case, we are justified under an emergency situation to confiscate whatever goods we deem necessary."

I almost grinned. "Glad to see you understand the urgency."

"How many people do you need? I can assign you one of the angels, and I have templars if you require fighting numbers."

"Having too many people going in might get us noticed. I'd rather use stealth. The vault is in a remote location, managed by Norway. It's on a fairly remote island, inside a sandstone mountain, supposed to be all kinds of disaster-proof. I'm going to assume security includes cameras and other deterrents."

"Sounds as if you'd have to be beamed outside this vault, as I doubt the cantorii can penetrate."

"Speaking of the cantorii, can it provide temporary storage at a specific temperature? The seeds are being kept at around minus eighteen or so Celsius. An optimum perseveration temperature. My plan is to first load up on edibles, herbs, vegetables, and fruits. Then if we have time and space, I'll grab other types that might help if terraforming is needed, like beneficial trees and grasses."

Metatron didn't look at me but rather had his head angled to look upward as he mused aloud. "The cantorii can store more than you think, and it might not be necessary for you to manually remove items for beaming aboard. We simply have to find a way for the cantorii to get a direct line inside."

"If we can get in." I'd heard conflicting reports on whether there were human guards or not. Plus rumors of booby traps, which sounded a little farfetched. That was the kind of thing you saw in movies, not in real life. "If we have to force our way inside, I'd like to do so without heedlessly hurting anyone." My intention wasn't to cause harm.

Metatron nodded in agreement. "I agree we should try for subtlety. A pity Elija refused your request. He is very good at stealth operations, but fret not, while not yet an archangel, Munna will be able to aid. I believe you two are relatively comfortable in each other's company, are you not?"

"We are," I replied with a nod. Munna was one of the friendlier angels who didn't intimidate given he lacked size and the warrior aura of some of the others. He tended to have a pleasant attitude unlike Elija who scowled a lot. Pity because he'd be gorgeous if he smiled once in a while.

"Great. I'll have him take you to the cantorii where you can brief him about this vault of seeds and plan how you'll infiltrate the facility. While you're doing that, I'm going to devise a way to beam the entire collection without moving a thing."

"You can do that?"

One corner of his mouth curved. "We will soon find out. So you worry about getting in, and I'll worry about the exiting part."

"When should I be ready to leave?"

"Now?" He arched a brow at me.

My mouth rounded. "Wow. Okay. Let me grab my notes on the vault, and I'll meet Munna…" I trailed off and waited for Metatron's answer.

"By the entrance as soon as you can get there. I will locate him at once and inform him of his new assignment."

I bounced on the balls of my feet. "Thank you."

"No need for thanks. We are allies in this endeavor."

All but Elija, I thought as I sprinted to my room to pack my notes and some spare clothes. I shouldn't be gone long if all went well, but I liked to be prepared. In the end, I took few clothes as I stuffed my bag with paper because I knew the cantorii didn't exactly have access to Earth's computer networks. While I ran around trying to get ready in a rush, I printed as much as I could about the Svalbard vault. It made for a lumpy bag that banged my hip as I hurried through the many passages making my way to the surface and the exit door. Not the giant aircraft-carrier-sized one—that looked like a mountain on the outside. We used the smaller side door, tucked under some strategically placed boulders.

In the chamber before the exit, I found Elija wearing a scowl.

He noticed my bag. "Going somewhere?"

"To the cantorii to rescue some seeds."

"You mean steal," he sneered.

"Actually, according to your boss, we're confiscating them under an emergency protocol. So not theft."

He frowned. "Metatron condones your mission?"

"He does, and he offered me help."

Elija's lips flattened. "Very well. We shall get your seeds."

I snorted. "Not we. You're off the hook. Metatron already hooked me up with an angel. I'm meeting him here."

"Hey Lulu, sorry I'm late," Munna declared, calling me by my nickname, before Elija had a chance to reply. The thick angel arrived wearing a harness around his torso, which had a leash coming out of it leading to a second mess of straps dangling in his hand. "I was just finishing up the work on this." He shook it in my direction.

"What is that?" I asked, holding the strap to my bag tight lest they see my trembling hands. I had a feeling I knew what Munna meant to do with me.

"I've designed a strap system to hold you in place during flight but leaves my hands free in case we are attacked."

Attacked?

My eyes widened. "Wait, is that a possibility? I thought the demons didn't know our location."

"They don't. But I like to be prepared." Munna offered the explanation with a wide grin.

Elija continued to grimace. "Why didn't you tell me you were working with her?"

I wondered at Munna's cool tone as he replied, "Because you didn't need to know." Then more pleasantly to me, "Ready?"

I nodded. "How do I strap myself in?"

"Get rid of the baggage first," Munna advised.

"It's my notes on the seed vault."

"I'll carry them," Elija growled, snagging the bag from my grip.

"Look at you doing something other than showing off your bad attitude," I exclaimed brightly.

It was totally worth it to see his intense glower as he stalked outside.

Munna snickered. "You've got a way of getting him riled."

"What can I say? We rub each other wrong. Now, how do we put on this bondage contraption?"

Munna showed me how to get into the harness, and I tried to not show my nervousness. While super cool—Holy hot chili sauce, I was about to fly—I really had to hope everything held or I'd splat on the ground.

We headed outside, me trailing like a reluctant puppy. It didn't help I had to shove my glasses in a pocket lest I lose them in flight. We emerged to find ourselves in late afternoon, the sun barely visible for the gray clouds.

Elija took one look at us bound together and shook his head. "Seems dangerous." With that comment, he launched himself. It didn't take long for him to be high in the sky.

"Ignore him. I built it solid. Ready?" Munna asked.

"Wondering if I should have thought this through a little longer," my muttered reply.

"Fear not, God won't let us fall," Munna declared before launching himself into the air. Given the slack in the tether between us, it took a second for me to follow with a jolt. I bit my tongue rather than squeak as my feet left the ground, the rising somewhat jerky as Munna strained to bring us straight up.

I tried to not think of the impossible physics that entailed. The power needed to propel not only his weight but mine from a stationary position. Was this what Munna meant about God not letting us fall?

I kept my eyes open to experience every second and saw the ground rapidly receding as he rose higher and higher. His mighty wings flapped, handling the weight against all scientific odds. It made no sense. The angels weren't any lighter than a human. As far as I could tell, they didn't have the hollow bones of birds, or less dense flesh and muscle. Yet illogical or not, it worked, and we flew.

The harness held me—for the moment. I dangled below Munna by a few feet, arms and legs spread, kind of like skydiving—without the falling part.

Elija coasted slightly ahead of us, leading the grumpy way. As to why we had to fly? Contacting the cantorii required using the HALO, the problem being the HALO acted as a beacon that would draw any demons in the vicinity. Now, there might not be any, and we were being over-cautious, but we couldn't take any chances.

We had two almost ready spaceships in the hangar below ground. Nothing could jeopardize their construction. So we moved away from it. High enough above the ground in the dimming cloud-filtered daylight that I couldn't see my shadow.

The sun had started to set as we climbed even higher, the air thin and cold, before we reached the nearest town. We did not want to be noticed. A thin misty cloud dampened my skin and gave me a shivering chill. The wisps of it made it hard to see far. Elija had disappeared from sight, and the only sound was the rush of air past my face.

When we burst above the cumulus layer, the light of the three-quarter moon hit me without a shred of warmth, but my shiver wasn't from the cold.

Munna said it before my brain could process what I saw flapping in front of us. "Imps."

They appeared just as surprised to see us, a flock of them ranging in size from large dog to steroid-bulked wrestler, hovering above the clouds and suddenly turning to eye us. Their faces were distorted versions of a human's, their bodies twisted, their skin mottled and lumpy, the wings leathery like a bat. The most fearsome thing about them? Their jagged claws and teeth. The flying monsters hissed as they spotted us.

I didn't need Munna's warning, "Stay tucked tight," to know I didn't want to be in anyone's way. The angel pulled his sword, and as it gleamed, I wondered where Elija had gotten to. We'd lost him in the clouds.

Then I had no time to think, as the imps attacked. Five in total, and they all darted in from every direction. My tether had me jerking and spinning as Munna met their challenge.

His blade rose, and swiped, digging into flesh and limb, his success evident in the squeals and the spray of blood. I wanted to close my eyes—violence was not my thing—yet I couldn't help but watch.

Watch as he fought, destroying the imps that attacked, looking like he'd win...

Then more of them suddenly rose from the clouds, screeching in rage, quite a few of them struggling due to wounds in their limbs and wings. The reason? The angel that followed. Elija emerged from the cumulus layer with his sword out and his eyes shining bright.

"Come back here for Elyon's judgment, foul beasts!" He exhorted them to return, and when they didn't, Elija tore after the imps with a fury and grace that stole the breath. Munna grunted, and we dropped a few feet. My eyes widened as I glanced upward to see a dark spot spreading on his usually snowy wings.

Blood.

The injury had him faltering, and we dipped again. The exposed vulnerability had the nearest pair of imps attacking. With shrill cries, they threw themselves at Munna.

His HALO suddenly ignited, driving the monsters back. I heard him say something in that melodic language the angels used, even as he gripped the tether to bring me close. The HALO flared brighter just as an imp threw himself at the tether with claws extended. It severed so quickly that, when Munna beamed out of sight, he did so without me, because I was falling!

CHAPTER 4

Elija sensed the imps in the clouds before they suddenly whipped past him, the leathery flap of their wings muffled by the thick moisture of the clouds.

No time to wonder where they came from or how they'd located them. Elija's blade emerged and went to work, his arm moving without conscious thought, severing the most logical places. A tendon in the wing. An entire reaching arm.

But there were too many of them.

And what of Munna with his human and useless cargo?

He shot upwards, emerging from the misty layer into a moonlight battle, Munna conducting himself in excellent form, their sparring practice on the long journey showing in his smooth moves.

Elija's arrival distracted his gaze for a moment.

"Pay attention," he yelled.

Too late did Munna notice the imp that dove from above. The blow struck Munna's wing, and his flight faltered. His human cargo didn't scream, but she did look on with wide eyes.

Munna's HALO ignited. He was going to beam out. Might as well. The imps knew they were here.

His own HALO illuminated in a burst of bright just as Munna disappeared.

And Cindy-lu fell!

Elija didn't ask to be placed aboard the cantorii. He dove, his wings tucking in tight as he arrowed in her direction. He had to move quick because the imps had noticed her freefalling and dropped to follow and taunt her on the way to her crash landing —and death.

This was his fault. Earlier he'd rejected her request. If he'd partnered with the strange plant doctor, she'd have been in his arms and safe.

She finally cried out as an imp grabbed her arm, digging in with its claws. She flailed and screeched, which only served to excite the imps and cause more to latch onto her. Elija had sheathed his sword before he dived and pulling it now would ruin his trajectory. Instead, he rounded his fingers and slammed into the first imp he encountered, tearing him from Cindy-lu, who gasped. He snagged the imp by the head and twisted sharply before rolling, using his rotation to find Cindy-lu and the remaining threat.

His HALO hummed, letting him know someone wanted to talk. *Not now.*

He spotted Cindy-lu, grappling with a single imp, screaming in its face as she dug her fingers into its head. As he neared, his extended wings giving him direction to glide, he noticed her gouging at its eyes.

Nice.

He couldn't help but admire her tenacity. He'd pictured her as someone who'd hide; after all, she lacked the size or muscle or weapon to do any harm.

Those tiny fingers could scratch though. The imp squealed and pushed away, too late. One eye gushed unhealthily. The remaining imp veered off as it spotted him.

He swept close to Cindy-lu and snared the whipping tether, using it to drag her to him, his wings backdrafting to slow their descent.

Her lips parted as he managed to draw her to his chest. She exhaled against him, "Holy fucking shit. Thank you for saving me."

Profane but heartfelt.

Maybe that was why he smiled in her hair. Hair that smelled nice. He turned his head, cleared his mind, and called the cantorii for transport.

Then answered the buzzing.

Munna erupted. "There you are. Cindy-lu is—"

He interrupted with a mental reply. "In my arms."

"You have her?" a baffled Munna asked.

"Yes. Coming aboard." Since she wasn't his responsibility, he brought her to Munna's quarters where they found him in the process of removing his shirt to deal with his wounds, the most grievous one being the torn ligament in his wing. Without a Jesus Christ on board, they no longer had access to God's healing touch. Only a Jesus could wield it, meaning they'd have to let their wounds follow a natural, and much slower, route.

Munna grimaced. "That was an unexpected surprise."

Elija set down the woman, who gasped, "Are we back aboard your spaceship?"

"Yes." A short reply. Elija's gaze took in the bleeding dropping to the floor from her arms. "You are injured."

"I'm fine," she muttered jamming her glasses on her face and peering around with interest.

"I'll get the supplies." Munna stomped to the wall, which projected a shelf with a jar filled with a healing salve, a basin of fluid for cleaning, a cloth for washing, and another for binding. There was also needle and thread.

"Right after I clean up the human—"

She interrupted. "Excuse me. I have a name. And

I can fix my own scratches." She stomped to Munna to swipe the cloth and began dabbing.

Elija left her to deal with her own injuries and went behind Munna to examine his wound. "They tore through and through. But it's straight, not jagged. I'll help you clean the wing and stitch it."

"You are the worst at it," Munna complained.

Cindy-lu, in the midst of winding cloth around her forearms, interjected. "I'm actually first aid certified and have sewn my fair share of things."

A pointing Munna said, "I'd rather take my chances with her."

"Go ahead." Elija could have left, but he remained. He couldn't have said why, even as his gaze tracked the woman—Cindy-lu—as she rinsed her cloth in the basin and then dabbed it at Munna's injury.

"You call your spaceship *can-tor-ee*, right?" she asked.

"Yes."

"Which I understand is indicative of its stage of development, after which it becomes an ark."

"Correct."

"What comes after an ark?"

Elija snorted. "Nothing."

"Really?"

"What else would there be?" Elija asked genuinely puzzled.

"I don't know. I was just curious. Is Heaven like a giant ark then? What about Hell?"

"Must you ask so many questions?" he complained as she threaded a needle.

She offered him a rigid glare. "This might be everyday blah for you, but being on an alien vessel is kind of epic for me."

"Hardly alien," was his indignant reply.

Her lips curved. "Not all that angelic either." She then looked away from him to finely stitch Munna's cut. She appeared gentle and adept as she wound the thread through and through, closing up the hole, giving it a tight seal.

When done, she smeared it with salve and then ordered Munna to, "Not move it for a few days at least. You want the flesh to heal, not continuously tear apart causing scar tissue. Assuming you scar, that is."

"We do when we don't have Heaven's healing available to us," Munna admitted. He would have reached for the discarded cloth to clean the rest of his wounds, but she snatched it first and began swabbing the puny scratches.

And Munna let her!

Elija couldn't stand watching as she rubbed salve into Munna's flesh.

Rather than snap for no reason, he growled, "I've things to attend to." Fists clenched, he stomped out of the room. He headed for his chambers and stripped the moment he entered. He'd not completely escaped unscathed. The satchel he'd managed to hold on to and forgotten went first. He'd have to return it to the little human.

Who'd valiantly fought an attack that should have never happened.

He cleansed and dressed before leaving for the Echo chamber to see what the cantorii might have detected. Nothing. Because the cantorii, not being omniscient, didn't know to look. The imps shouldn't have been there.

No one knew they were leaving. No one except for Metatron, and Elija refused to believe the man set them up. Who else did that leave aware of their plans?

Anyone who watched them go if he were to be honest. The humans did love their cameras, and he'd not realized just how pervasive and intrusive they could be until he'd watched some footage.

Could there be a traitor at the base?

Munna entered the Echo chamber as the idea occurred, disrupting him.

Elija tuned out the angelic version of a database. "Was there something you needed?"

"I'm afraid this"—Munna glanced at his injured wing—"is going to be a problem."

"Don't worry. It will heal nicely. Her stitching is quite tight and good."

"It is, and I'm not worried about functionality

once it's healed, but now I can't fly, meaning I can't help, not for the physical parts at any rate. Someone has to take my place." Munna stared at him.

For a second, Elija thought about saying no. He couldn't do it.

Why not?

Metatron had countenanced it. The Atlantis expected it. Humanity needed it.

Why did he hesitate?

Oh yeah, because God wanted Eden to die.

Even the loyal Elija had to admit it seemed drastic. And really, helping Cindy-lu retrieve some seeds wasn't the worst thing he could be doing.

"I'll aid the human."

"Don't be so excited. And you know she has a name, right?" Munna asked with an arch of his brow.

"Yes, I know her name. Cindy-lu."

"Her friends call her Lulu," Munna informed. "A nickname her dad gave her."

A simple derivative, but it suited her. Short and perky like her. But why had Munna known that information? He cast a glance in the other warrior's direction, wondering exactly how close he and the human were. Then he asked himself, *why do I care?*

Maybe he shouldn't do this.

Before he could turn coward, Elija said, "Tell her I'll deal with her after I've studied our target and devised a plan."

"Tell her yourself. She's in your chambers."

Elija's jaw dropped. "Why my room?"

"Because I knew you'd do the right thing, and now that she's your responsibility, seems only right she stay with you."

"No. She can't!" he huffed.

"Why not?"

A mental struggle ensued as Elija sought an excuse. Anything that wasn't a lie. He had nothing but, "She discomfits me."

The admission caused Munna to grin. "I'm aware. It's because she's forthright and not at all in awe of you."

"She's stubborn and says very inappropriate things."

"To you. In her society, she is quite normal," Munna pointed out.

"Because they're savages." His muttered complaint.

"They're a flock that needs our help. Or have you decided you no longer have the flock's interest at heart?"

"What of God's command?"

"You and I both know the command is too harsh."

It was. Hence why he sighed. "I said I'd help her." A begrudging acceptance.

"Try to be nice while you do it. She doesn't deserve to deal with the grumpy version of you."

"I'm not grumpy," he groused. Okay, maybe a little. Not his usual demeanor. Blame Cindy-lu. Little Lulu truly did put him off kilter.

"I'll work on a new harness for her."

An offer that had Elija quickly saying, "No need. I think I'd prefer to hold on to her myself. Besides, I don't plan to be in the air long." He'd have the cantorii drop them as close as possible to this secure location.

"Metatron did say to not leave until I'd spoken to him. In this case, now you. He's working on something to ease the transfer of the seeds."

"Anything else?"

"Just to get in with as little damage as possible."

A stealth mission? Elija excelled at those. "I can't believe I'm going to be a farmer," he groused. Seeds were plants. Farmers tended those.

"More like a shepherd, seeing as how your actions will be keeping the humans alive for their journey and implantation."

"Against Elyon's wishes," he reminded.

"I don't care." Munna pursed his lips. "That command goes against our creed of doing no harm and preserving the flock."

"Unless there's rot inside. Once it spreads, everything is tainted." He'd learned that in the creche.

"I don't think humans are rotten," Munna defended.

"They are far from peaceful, though. They are violent and destructive."

"Also artistic and loving. And they cook up the most delicious food." Munna's eyes almost rolled back in remembered pleasure.

"They're interesting," Elija conceded. "In this case, I do wonder if perhaps God might be hasty and later regret the decision."

"And if he doesn't?" Munna pinned him with a stare.

"I doubt I'll care once he smites me," his sarcastic rejoinder.

Munna laughed. "He'd have to leave his castle first. Now go, find Lulu and stop looking at her as a human but as a person."

"It would be easier if she didn't talk so much," he groaned.

"You'll live, brother." Munna slapped him on the back in the guise of guiding him to the exit from the Echo chamber.

A coward would have avoided his quarters. Elija walked in head held high and braced. He didn't know what he expected. Certainly not Cindy-lu sitting cross-legged on his bed, ignoring him for the sheets of paper scattered around her.

"What are you doing?" he barked.

She lifted her head and smiled at him. "Looking for a way inside."

CHAPTER 5

THE MOMENT ELIJA ENTERED HE LOOKED AS IF HE'D sucked on something sour. "You made a mess."

I glanced at my notes spread out around me on his bed. "Your table was too small."

"There is a better way to organize these." He began snatching the sheets one by one, his HALO active as he turned them fully around before setting each page down and doing the same to the next.

I bounced on the bed and clasped my hands. I knew exactly what he did, as Tamara had told me about it. He was having his HALO copy my notes, which would then, in turn, allow us to access them holographically while on his ship. My reaction showed off my geek. I was okay with it.

The moment he finished, I squeaked, "Show me."

He shook his head but twisted his hand, and

there were my notes, suspended in the air, holographic versions. I squealed. "This is awesome." Manipulating them proved faster and more organized. I stood and began flipping my sheets around. Known security measures. Rumors of. Images of the seed vault from the outside. Aerial views of the area.

Svalbard Vault resided on an island. Not impossible to reach, but difficult. Those entering needed Visas giving permission. Tourism being one of the more common reasons because of the excellent view of the night skies and its light shows from there.

It was also a barren place, with less than fifty miles of road on the whole island. It had an airport, even a hotel or two depending on the season. Camping was what most people chose to do for the full experience, that and trekking up the sandstone mountain to see the mouth of vault.

Elija stood not far away and gazed upon all my notes before pointing at an image showing the narrow sliver front of the building. "This is the only entrance?"

"As far as I know, yes."

He frowned. "It is very exposed."

"I'm aware."

He enlarged it to look at the doorway. "Locked, I assume?"

"Most definitely. And I'd wager on an alarm if we force it open. Beyond it, I have no idea what to expect."

He eyed me and shook his head. "It seems like an elaborate setup for seeds."

"A seed is life."

"This will be fraught with issues. The moment we beam in, we're vulnerable to attack."

"The imps can't find us if you keep your HALO turned off."

"I am no longer sure of that," he murmured. "I've yet to ascertain if the imps we encountered were by chance or design."

"Not another traitor!" I huffed. First, it turned out my original boss when the angels landed, Mr. A, AKA Astaroth, was a demon prince who kidnapped a bunch of his employees to work on his diabolical plan to bring Hell to Earth. He was abetted by a coworker of mine, Bruce, who deserved everything bad that happened to him. Another who couldn't resist the temptation of the dark side? Jesus, God's own scion, who tried to sabotage our evacuation efforts.

"It could be a coincidence," he stated without much conviction.

"So we need to be quiet about our actions is what you're saying. Got it. Does that mean keeping my lips zipped around Munna?"

"He wouldn't betray us to the enemy. Not after the way his lover died," Elija announced casually. It surprised. I mean, I knew the angels weren't these pure sexless beings. Lilith practically blushed when she alluded to Aziel's prowess and explained they were actually encouraged to have sex and make babies. It was another thing to realize angels looked for more than carnal pleasures—they had relationships and could love. Lilith with Aziel and Tamara with Zakai were proof.

"Where should we teleport?" I asked, running my finger on the map. "Here's the vault." I pointed. "This is the airport. Lots of signals there if you think it will help hide our presence."

"An airport means people. I can't exactly hide what I am." He ruffled his feathers.

I cocked my head. "It's really inconvenient how God made it so you can't blend in. I mean, if it wasn't for the wings, you'd look like one of us."

He recoiled as if the idea repugned. Jerk. "My wings are not an attachment to be removed at will." An indignant reply.

I could have been more sensitive. "Sorry. It's just it makes no sense to me since I heard they're a genetic modification given by God."

I could see he wanted to deny it. In the end, he managed a stiff, "Our ability to fly is Elyon's blessing."

"Like the HALOs that attract demons?" I couldn't help a lilt of sarcasm. "Seems to me like he could have done more to ensure you fit in if he wanted you to spread his word."

"Other flocks have respect for Elyon's Warriors

and do not question everything they are told," he huffed in annoyance.

I remained undaunted. "Miffed we're too smart to fall to our knees in blind worship?"

"It would have been easier," he muttered.

"Sorry to disappoint. Now back to the plan. Since the airport is a bad idea, we land somewhere in the boonies." I swept my finger across the map. "But not too far out because we'll need supplies if we're going to hike into the mountain."

"Or we could land right outside its door," he suggested.

I zoomed the image. "In plain sight? It's like you want us to fail."

"We could go at night."

"Even better. Let's tackle unknown security in the dark."

"What do you suggest then?" he growled.

"We set up a campsite close to the mountain where no one will see the winged man. I'll join a tourist group and trek up the mountain to get a peek at the door. I should be able to handle it." I hoped. I'd read it was four hours. I remained unclear if that was one-way or round trip.

"What is a campsite?" he queried.

"A shelter, to rest and regroup."

"I just need a stout branch," he remarked.

"I'd rather not fall out of a tree."

"I guess you are rather clumsy."

I made a face at him. "More like I prefer a bed, something flat, on the ground."

"I assume you'll want supplies to sustain yourself. I know your kind are more fragile when it comes to nutrition and temperature."

"Excuse me for needing to eat and drink." I rolled my eyes. "Yes, I will need rations and water. Warm clothing as well. While the outside temp isn't horrid currently at around minus ten, the vault is kept at sub eighteen to twenty Celsius."

"And what do we need to get inside?"

"I don't know yet."

"Your plan is overly complicated. While I agree we should land out of sight, there's no need to waste so much time. Not when I have relics to get us past traps and avoid observation."

"Wait, when you say relics, what does that mean?" Because I'd seen the Indiana Jones movies and I knew what I'd like it to entail.

He stared at me before sighing. "You'll ask me questions until I explain, won't you? And then you'll insist on me showing you."

I grinned. "Why, Eli, I do believe you're getting to understand me."

"Terrifying," was his dry reply as he led me out of his room into a hall that appeared rather boring and seamless. The first time I'd been aboard, right after they rescued us from Mr. A, I'd not had time to explore. I'd also known very little about the ship—including the fact that it was living.

I couldn't help but run my fingers on the surface and would have sworn I felt a shiver then a gentle pulse. "I still can't believe the cantorii are alive. Do they have to be trained to do their job?"

"In a sense. When they become large enough, they begin taking angels on flights. As they mature and have more space, more crew are added, as well as more expectation placed on them, which develops functionality."

"Sounds kind of cold given it's alive."

"You are thinking of it in human terms. An ark, given its longevity, matures slowly."

"Can it speak to you?"

"Some claim an ark will evolve cognizance over time."

"What do you think?"

"That we'll find out when the Atlantis returns. I don't believe there's ever been one as ancient as it."

The mention of age had me blurting out, "How old are you?"

"In terms you'd understand? More years than you could imagine. But less than most. I am considered young compared to many."

"You don't age." I stated rather than asked.

"No, although our bodies can deteriorate. A return to Heaven rejuvenates us that we might continue to serve."

"Munna says Jesus Christ used to be your healer. He shaved like a decade off of Lilith to prove a point. Took some off Tamara too. Does he have all of Elyon's powers to wield?"

"No, and what Jesus did have was but a pale shadow of God's full might."

"Have you met God?"

"Not in person but he's presided over events I've participated in."

"He must be pretty awesome for you to follow him without knowing him personally."

"He is God."

"And?" I couldn't help but question. "What makes him so special that angels have to listen to him? Why should humans?"

"Because he ensured your kind would achieve sentience."

"Only so we could make some epic soul juice for him to use to perform his miracles. Don't deny it. Lilith and Tamara explained it to me. Your God is like the owner of some land with raw minerals, and angels are his coal miners, harvesting it, putting themselves in harm's way so he can benefit."

I'd been very much against "the man" and capitalism in my college days. Then I'd started seeing the way shared collectives always broke down without structure. How the brightest left, headhunted with promises of more money and perks. Me? I was lured from the ethically sourced lab where

I'd been working for peanuts by promises of state-of-the-art equipment and carte blanche when it came to designing a food system fit for space, as well as establishing crops once we reached a barren planet. At the time Mr. A spoke of reaching Mars or even playing around with Venus.

"God takes only so he can give to us all. Without him, there would be no heaven, no arks, no ships at all." Elija had drunk the propaganda, but I couldn't help but question.

"Is Hell, like, the same only supposedly the evil version?"

"Not supposedly. They are evil. They don't allow planets to thrive but strip them of everything they want."

"Seems counterproductive. What if they one day run out of planets to rape?"

"Hasn't happened yet," he advised.

"Neither has your God putting a stop to their pillaging," I pointed out. "Guess we shouldn't count on your him to send any miracles to help Earth in this, our time of need."

"What do you think the relics are?" he announced, placing his hand on the wall, a seemingly innocuous spot and yet it glowed before dissolving into a doorway. He stepped in first, and then I followed, immediately gasping.

"Holy crap." I knew some people who would have creamed themselves at what I saw.

Racks holding weapons of extreme craftsmanship and beauty. A sword four feet long, with a pommel too big even for even Elija's large hand. Daggers with the ends looking as if they'd been dipped in tar.

I didn't need his murmured, "Don't touch anything. Some of the relics are poisoned," to keep my hands to myself. I did a circuit of the room, noticing objects that made no sense, like the basket of differently-sized glass spheres or the deep chest, which he opened, containing nothing. Yet he reached in and pretended to put something out.

Then swirled his hands and disappeared!

CHAPTER 6

Elija gave her no warning when he placed the cloak of shielding over his body and disappeared from her sight.

Her mouth rounded as big as her eyes. "You've got an invisibility shield!" she squeaked. "That is so cool."

Her pleasure pleased a little too much. He whirled the fabric off his shoulders and revealed himself to say, "It's actually a cloak, not a shield. It's considered the best form to allow it to be encompassing but also easy to shed.

"How does it work?" She reached and brushed his flesh, causing a tingle that had him sucking in a breath. He quickly thrust the object she sought into her grip.

"The cloak was blessed by God."

"Magic," she breathed.

He didn't correct her because, to someone like her, it would seem mysterious and strange. To him, the use of suul to give power to an object had always been commonplace.

She ran the fabric through her fingers, holding it over her hand and watching it disappear. "What happens if you put it down and forget where it is?" she asked, glancing at him.

"It sometimes gets lost," he admitted. "Some will leave signaling devices with their cloak when they remove it to prevent that from happening."

"This is perfect for getting close to the vault."

"With one problem. Given its billowy nature, it doesn't work during flight."

"That's fine. We can hike up the mountain completely invisible and close to the vault without triggering any cameras," she exclaimed with excitement.

"We only have one cloak at the moment, though."

"Big enough for two. Put it back on a second, would you."

He snared it for a whirl over his shoulders, only stiffening a bit as she tucked herself close. The fabric enclosed them, but that wasn't the reason for the warmth infusing his body.

"It might be awkward to climb, but if we go at night, we won't have to resort to using it until we reach the vault area." She slipped away and turned a shining face on him. "What other treasures do you have in here?" She whirled to look around.

He stowed the cloak and then gave her a tour. "These are somnolence spheres." He pointed to the glass bulbs. "When shattered, it releases a gas that puts everything in the vicinity to sleep for a period of time."

"How far does it spread?"

"Depends on the size." He pointed out the various balls of gas that ranged from small, and fitting the palm of his hand, to the one that needed both to handle it.

"Does it put angels to sleep?"

"Anyone who gets too close, which is why we apply the antidote first." He pulled open a pouch hanging on the bin of spheres to show her the tiny vials. "A few drops on the tongue protects for longer than the gas lasts."

"We'll need some of those sleep bombs to put any guards inside, or out for that matter, to sleep. Got anything to put electronic alarms to bed? Maybe an EMP pulse?"

He pursed his lips. "I'm unsure of your meaning."

"There will be cameras, motion detectors, a screaming alarm, something on that door. It needs to be disabled."

"Run on electricity?" he queried aloud as he glanced around.

"Yes."

"I have something for that." He went to a peg with hanging amulets and selected one with a dark stone.

"A necklace?" She injected a dubious tone into the query.

"That absorbs electrical current. Useful on planets where the storms can be unpredictable and lively."

"I don't know… I mean, the wires will be hidden."

"Doesn't matter. It only requires proximity to absorb."

"I'll take your word for that. Now the only dilemma is getting inside."

"That's easy." He pulled his divinii blade. "This can cut through any metal or stone."

"Are you sure? It would suck to get all the way to the vault, only to realize your sword isn't long enough to go through the door."

He eyed the length of the weapon. "You think the barrier is thicker?"

"I think we need to be prepared just in case."

He glanced around at the various objects—spears capable of piercing even the stoutest chitin, armor to deflect, footwear that could make it seems as if someone walked on air, a portable HALO given to allies to create a conduit for communication. Many wondrous things but the object he settled on…

He grabbed a shield with a mirror-like surface. "This might work."

She pursed her lips. "I doubt the door will care if you show it its reflection."

"It's actually a mirror of uncreation. Once activated, whatever is reflected will revert to its earliest origin."

"So the metal door will become metal ore?" Her nose wrinkled.

"Actually, everything begins as dust."

Her eyes widened. "Ooh. That's kind of cool."

An expression he'd come to understand meant she approved. "Its drawback is its unwieldiness."

"Speaking of unwieldy, are you going to be able to carry all this stuff?"

"I will find a way. Munna might have a solution. He's crafty in that respect."

"What you need is a bottomless bag."

At his blank look, she added, "It's a fictional thing we see in literature and movies. It's basically a bag, or a closet, a storage space that is infinity bigger on the inside than out."

He frowned. "That is impossible."

"Unless you use magic."

"Unfortunately, we have nothing like that on board, and we'd need God or, at the very least, a Jesus Christ to even try."

"Pity. And that leads me to the next question. How are we going to get the seeds out and onboard your ship? I assume there will be some machinery or hand carts inside. We'll have to do several trips. Have you talked to Metatron? He'd said he would take care of the exit strategy."

"I will converse with him before our departure."

"Which is when? An hour? Two?"

"We will rest first before embarking on our mission." He led her from the chamber of relics to his quarters, whereupon she frowned.

"Your bed doesn't look big enough for the two of us. Unless you like to cuddle. Even if you don't, I should warn you, I am clingy in my sleep. I have a body pillow at home that I strangle at night."

He only understood part of what she said. He quickly clarified any misconceptions she might hold. "You will get the mattress. I will perch for the night." He pointed to the mount by the bed.

She cocked her head. "You're going to roost like a bird, for real? And here I thought Lilith was pulling my leg when she told me Aziel liked to do that."

"How else would we sleep?"

"Sprawled, of course." She showed him by throwing herself onto the mattress, arms and legs akimbo. It resulted in the fabric of her pants tightening over her buttocks and outlining its shape.

"If I did that, there would be no room for you."

She rolled to her back to reply. "You'd be surprised. I'm like a python when it comes to wrapping myself around things while I sleep."

"Isn't that a snake that crushes its prey to death?" He'd come across it during his Earth studies.

"It just likes to hug." She winked. "Got any pajamas? I packed everything but," she admitted with a sheepish shrug.

"Pajamas are..."

"Comfortable clothing to wear to sleep."

"Like a breechcloth?"

"Um... Not sure that will be enough coverage. I have boobs, remember?" She gestured to the swelling at her chest. Her bosom was much more pronounced than the few female angels he'd met during his brief visits to Heaven. Their mammary glands tended to be less pronounced, as the angelic host had moved away from chest feeding, calling it barbaric and outdated. But most colonized planets still tended to feed their young from their own flesh.

"Why must your chest be covered?" He didn't understand, seeing as how he removed his shirt all the time. The only reason he wore a breechcloth was because it kept his nether parts from swinging in the field where something might try and bite them.

"On Earth, many consider them objects of sexual desire." Her cheeks turned a pinkish hue that signaled embarrassment.

"Why?" He was honestly baffled.

She huffed. "Because. Anyhow, I am not sleeping in just underpants. Do you have a loose shirt I can borrow?"

Apparently, the cantorii had something better. The wall opened and revealed a pile of fabric. She pulled it free and shook it out exclaiming, "A nightgown. Perfect. Turn around."

"Why?"

"So I can change, duh."

He didn't understand why, but he did as asked, turning to remove his own garments for comfort. His shirt came off his upper body, and his boots went next, as did his trousers. The fabric items went into a hole in the wall, where the cantorii would cleanse and return them. His boots were lined neatly alongside the sheath for his blade.

By the time he finished, Cindy-lu declared, "I'm decent. You can look."

He turned around to see her in a garment of thin material that clung to the tips of her mammary glands, outlining them in a way that had him thinking of what she'd said about them as sources of sexual pleasure. While he'd indulged in carnal activities a few times with others, he'd never gazed upon their frame as a source of enticement. They stimulated him, they copulated, and it was done.

Was it different on Earth? He'd not really delved into that aspect, mostly concerning himself with their military capability, weapons, and previous accounts of war.

Her eyes widened upon seeing him. "Goodness, you're a muscly fellow."

He glanced down at his body. "A soldier needs to be strong."

"And big," she muttered, her gaze straying lower, her cheeks once more turning a different shade before she turned her head. "Night, Elija." She crawled onto the bed and threw herself down, flipping side to side before huffing, "I don't suppose you have any pillows and blankets."

"You are cold?"

"I told you I like to snuggle in my sleep." She shrugged.

He went to the cantorii wall, and it opened yet again to provide what she'd asked for, which led to more questions.

"Just how well supplied is your ship? And how is it that it can locate the items in question and have them available to you almost instantly?"

"The cantorii provides what we require. The only supply it needs is of atrayla, which feeds it."

"Wait, are you saying it's conjuring these items? Like a replicator?"

His brow creased. "I'm not sure what that means."

"Your ship is basically creating stuff out of nothing."

"Out of astrayla," he corrected.

"Just like a replicator in a sci-fi movie, only your ship is alive. And amazing." She reached down to stroke the floor.

"What are you doing?" he asked as he dumped her requested items, which had a plushness to them that he'd never partaken of. In the shelter underground, he'd chosen to perch on the headboard of the bed to sleep.

"Saying thank you." She patted the floor. "Thank you, cantorii. Which, by the way, seems like a rude thing to call such a wondrous creature."

"It will attain a name when it ascends to ark status."

"Really?" she drawled. "And do you only name your children when they reach adulthood?"

"Of course not. Upon hatching, they are assigned an identity."

"And you don't see the disconnect?"

He pursed his lips. "It's how it's done."

"Doesn't make it right. It deserves a name."

"Then give it one," he snapped, not liking her logic because he understood it. Why did the cantorii have to wait to be named?

"That would be presumptuous." She leaned down low to the floor and whispered, "I'm sure you've been thinking of something, and I hope you'll tell me what it is."

With that said, she then curled against a pillow, while her head lay on a second, the blanket over top. He observed her from his perch, heard the soft evening of her breath as she relaxed.

And still, he stared. She confused him. Not only

because of her expressions and mannerisms but because of how she made him feel. Her near presence caused a stirring in his loins. Unusual for him. Perhaps he needed to take care of himself, even as long lapses didn't usually cause an issue.

Wondering what it would be like to indulge in carnal acts with a human, he fell asleep and into the nightmare he refused to acknowledge when awake.

That of the time he disobeyed God's command —and angels died.

CHAPTER 7

A GRUNT WOKE ME.

I twisted on the bed to find the source and did a double take in the dim lighting of the room. Elija perched for real on a strange contraption that reminded me of a swing, suspended from the ceiling, with a flat board for his feet. He was crouched, his arms tucked around his knees, his face pillowed on them. His wings draped behind.

He groaned again, and his entire frame shivered.

Did angels dream? If yes, his didn't appear too pleasant. Seemed more like a nightmare, seeing as how he winced and trembled. I rose from his bed and approached, slowly and carefully. Waking someone up in the midst of a deep sleep could be hazardous. I'd known a guy at work who did it after his girlfriend missed her alarm and got slugged for his trouble.

I spoke his name softly. "Elija?"

He shook his head and spoke, the words not any I recognized but melodious to the ear.

"You're having a bad dream." I kept talking to him, hoping he'd wake.

He rocked on the swing, his wings lifting and fluttering, his muscles tensing.

"Elija!" I spoke his name loudly, and he suddenly snapped awake, his eyes wide and unseeing as his hands reached and grabbed hold of me, lifting me from the floor to bring me face to face with him as he growled in his strange language.

I should have been scared. He outweighed and outmuscled me, and he had a hold of me by the arms tight enough I couldn't move my hands.

"Wake up!"

Rather than open his eyes, he drew me close, still murmuring, his tone low and pleading. It didn't take a translation to understand whatever he imagined hurt.

Since shouting didn't seem to work, I tried something a little more personal.

The mere inches between us meant I only had to lean a little to kiss his moving lips. They stilled. I kept my mouth pressed against his, and they parted on a warm exhalation. He'd yet to release me, or wake. I had my eyes open watching.

I softly slid my lips against his in a caressing

emotion, and the tension eased from him. He went from holding me aggressively to tucking me to his chest and taking over the kiss. He teased my lips, sucking the lower one gently.

The embrace aroused, and I couldn't help but moan, a small sound that had him suddenly going rigid before setting me on the floor, where I wavered, my lips tingling, and so I saw when he opened his eyes.

"What is going on?" his husky query.

"You were having a nightmare and wouldn't wake."

"Was not," he huffed, bristling at my statement.

"You were. I tried waking you, but you reacted badly and grabbed hold of me. Since I didn't know what to do to free myself, I kissed you."

"Kissed me..." Repeated as he lifted his fingers to his lips. His brows drew together tight. "You should not have done that."

Probably not, seeing as how I'd not asked permission. Rather than apologize, though, I changed the subject. "What were you dreaming about?"

"Nothing," a harsh reply.

"Didn't seem like nothing. It's also completely natural. Often times, our dreams make us relive our worst anxieties and fears. Weird considering you'd think our subconscious would want us to forget."

"Sometimes we need a reminder of the lessons we've learned," his abrupt reply as he leaped from the perch.

"And what lesson is that?"

"Never disobey God's will." He whirled from me and headed for the wall, reaching before it even opened. He plucked garments from within.

"Where are you going?"

"Metatron's onboard. I'm going to go speak with him before we depart." He dressed quickly and left me bemused and wondering what haunted the beautiful angel.

I'd just finished dressing, clothes appearing on a shelf that projected from the wall, when the door to his room opened, not to reveal Elija, but Munna.

I smiled. "Good morning. How's the wing doing?"

He grimaced. "Sore but healing cleanly thanks to your aid."

"A hospital would be better equipped to check for damage I missed," I reminded. He'd refused the day before when I told him I wasn't a proper nurse.

"I will be fine. Where is Elija?"

"Gone off in a snit. He had a bad dream, and it left him in a mood," I exclaimed.

"Let me guess, he denied having it?" Munna arched a brow, and I nodded.

"Yeah, claimed he didn't dream, but then he said

something weird about it being a reminder of things he shouldn't forget."

Munna's jaw tightened. "Because he refuses to let it go."

"You know why he's got nightmares?"

"Yes, but it is not my place to say anything other than it was a tragedy that he's chosen to take the blame for."

"Was he at fault?"

Munna shook his head. "There was no averting the disaster. He thinks a choice he made led to it. However, the outcome was inevitable."

"We are our own worst enemies sometimes," I muttered. Anxiety could be a cruel mistress. While not something I'd suffered often, I'd had my moments of self-doubt, mostly when I allowed what others said and thought of me to affect my decisions and actions. It took me getting to a point where I decided to say "screw it" before I realized I didn't care if people liked me or not. *I* liked me. I had faith in my decision-making abilities, and so long as I could live with my conscience, then I knew I was making the right choice.

"Very wise words for someone who's not lived as long as others." He winked at me. "Now, the reason I'm here is in regard to transporting you and some of the relics you'll be bringing on your trip."

"When did Elija contact you about that?" I'd been with him in the relic room and afterwards.

"He informed me earlier via the HALO that he is bringing the mirror and other items for this next trip. He wanted to know if I had any suggestions for transporting everything, including you, in one trip. Before you worry, given the failure of my last harness system, he's forbidden me from even suggesting another."

"It would have worked if not for the imps."

He grimaced. "I should have taken them into account. Anyhow, back to his request. I regret to inform he cannot carry the supplies and you at the same time. The mirror alone will make it unwieldy, and it is simply too much bulk."

"Elija's not a packhorse. I'm perfectly capable of carrying some things, and if the cantorii sets us on the ground, he doesn't have to fly me anywhere. We can walk to the vault."

"Walk?" Obviously not the answer he'd expected.

"The island is not a place where you can easily get around with a car. Residents usually boat in the warm months, snowmobile in the cold. There are some tourist buses that get close to the vault, but I doubt Elija would agree to board one. Not to mention, they'll go in the daytime when we're most likely to be noticed. Even at night, we'll have to be careful, as tourists like to flock to it and take pictures given its artistic design."

"If walking, you'll need packs comfortable for carrying," Munna mused aloud. "Do you have a full list of your equipment?"

"Not exactly but here's a quick list." I ticked things off on my fingers. "The relics, of course, mirror, glass bomb, necklace of electricity sucking, antidote so we don't snore. I'll be wearing my warm gear, but in case of emergency, we should have a tent, sleeping bag, and emergency food rations."

He frowned. "I don't know if I can acquire the last few on the cantorii, as they are not items we are familiar with. Let me see what I can do."

"Do we need to worry about imps?" Not something I thought I'd ever say aloud.

"I'd like to say no."

"But?" I prodded.

Munna's lips flatted. "It is possible they've found a way to track us even with the HALOs inactive, meaning you'll have to be careful."

"Would it help if the cantorii beamed us somewhere with a lot of airwaves? There is a small airport on the island, which will have lots of signal noise that might conceal our arrival."

"The idea is sound; however, it will be hard for Elija to move around in a busy place," Munna remarked.

"Not if he's wearing his cloak. The biggest issue would be getting from the airport to the mountain.

It's a fair distance to walk, and he won't fit into a car."

"But you do have larger vehicles called vans and busses? I've been researching, and they have the room within for someone with wings and the relics."

"A bus would have the size, but I don't know how to get Elija on board even if cloaked." I gnawed my thumb. "We could look at renting a van, but that creates a trail since they'll probably want identification and a credit card." I didn't know just how deep Astaroth's resources went. Could he track me via electronic methods?

"The cantorii can create identification and money for you," Munna reminded. "But let's look at this another way. If you didn't have to worry about Elija, what would you do?"

My lips curved. "Depending on how much snow is on the ground? Most likely a snowmobile. It can carry my gear, isn't reliant on their meager road system, and can get me close to the mountain before I have to hike in. But I can't see Elija holding on to me, riding on the back, which leads me to the question, how do your wings handle the cold?"

"Temperature is not an issue for us, usually. And you are right. He won't like relying on you to get to this mountain."

"Which is sexist," I muttered.

"Is it?" Munna shrugged. "Regardless of gender, you're an Earth human, and he is an Angel warrior who's used to being the one in charge and leading the way."

"Except that won't work this time. So my proposal is, the cantorii drops me there during daylight hours and I pretend I'm a tourist. If the cantorii can provide me with cash I can rent a snowmobile and gear."

"What of Elija?"

"The cantorii drops him at night when he won't be seen. He can then fly to meet me either at the base of the mountain so we hike together or at the top."

"I don't think he'll like that plan," Munna predicted.

"What plan?" Elija barked, stalking back in with a glower that went right to Munna. "What are you doing? You were supposed to be working on a carrying system, and yet here you are, empty-handed."

"I was getting more details from Lulu." Munna gestured. "She made some suggestions to avoid being noticed."

I let Munna explain the airport idea and how the many signals might mask our arrival. When we got to the part of the snowmobile being used as transport, he shushed us to have the cantorii conjure a hologram of the machine.

Elija's brows rose. "You cannot seriously expect me to ride one of those."

"You don't have to," I pipped in. "You'll be flying with some of the relics once it gets dark enough so you won't be noticed by casual observers. I'll be driving the snowmobile with the rest of our supplies to a spot we'll pick on the map beforehand."

"You can navigate in the dark?" he asked me.

"Probably not, which is why I'm going to do my part during daylight hours. I'll set up a campsite where you can easily find me. Once we meet up, we'll go up the mountain together."

He immediately argued, but not for the reason I would have assumed. "If I am left behind, then who will protect you?"

"Me," I countered. "I know how to shoot a gun." Though I'd have to add it to my list of requested supplies.

His lips pursed. "Long-range weapons are against God's will."

"You seem to forget I don't follow his commands. I'm going to help my race, not your God." I didn't couch my words.

He bristled and puffed his chest. "I thought you wanted to succeed."

"I will, whether you help me or not. Now, are you done arguing, or am I doing this alone?"

"I don't like your attitude," he growled.

"Ditto," I fired back.

"I could go instead of Elija." Munna cleared his

throat. "I'd be willing to ride behind you, thus negating the need to fly. My legs work fine."

Elija turned his head so fast in Munna's direction I worried he'd have whiplash. "You are to stay aboard and heal. I will go."

"And follow the plan?" I prodded.

"Maybe," was his ominous reply.

CHAPTER 8

Elija exited his room angry. He couldn't have explained the exact cause if anyone asked, though.

Entering to see Munna had been collaborating with Cindy-lu and concocting a scheme that put her on the surface without protection started his annoyance. Add in the fact she seemed absolutely determined to follow her plan despite Elija's reservations, plus Munna's offer to take Elija's place...

He seethed as he entered the relic room. As he gathered the supplies for their trip, he tried to calm himself, but it proved impossible, especially given the meeting he'd had with Metatron.

"I hear Munna had to step aside from the mission and that you're taking over," Metatron stated without welcome as Elija entered his quarters.

"Yes, I agreed to step in."

"Are you sure? Because if you have an issue with it, I can assign Eoch instead."

Elija frowned. "No need. I will aid the human."

"It's more than just aiding her. This task is about ensuring humanity has a chance to escape and start over." Left unspoken? The fact that this was against Elyon's orders and Elija had good reason to avoid such a situation... again.

His lips flattened.

"You have a problem with that?" Metatron asked softly.

"No." He didn't have a problem aiding Cindy-lu. The mission to retrieve seeds was trivial in the grand scheme of things. It was everything else that he remained conflicted about.

"But?"

Elija sighed. He couldn't go on avoiding the conversation with his principality forever. "By aiding them, we are in direct defiance of God."

"Let me ask you, does it seem right to let them die?"

"It feels wrong," Elija admitted with a roll of his shoulders. *"But—"*

"But nothing. I recently received a report from the Atlantis and found this planet has gone through a few cleansings already. Floods. Famines. Pestilence. Volcanoes. All of them acts of God."

"He must have had his reasons."

"The question is, were they valid? From what I've been able to discern, Elyon has tried to wipe out

humanity numerous times because they just wouldn't conform to his wishes. Despite his efforts, humanity has prevailed. Of all the flock planets, they are the most tenacious. Their evolution has rendered them the most advanced of all the seeded worlds."

Elija pursed his lips. "You sound as if you admire them."

"Because I do. They encourage innovation. They aren't afraid to explore and question."

"They build weapons to kill. They are depraved toward one another." Elija had read enough of the crimes to be appalled.

"Good and evil in one place. Balancing each other."

Elija frowned. "That doesn't sound like a good thing."

"Why? Because it's not how we've been taught? Did you ever wonder about the galaxies we are forbidden from entering?"

"No. They are obviously too dangerous, and God wishes to preserve our lives."

"Spoken like a proper soldier. What if I were to tell you the forbidden galaxies had intelligent species within them? Beings that have made it clear they will have nothing to do with Heaven or Hell and attempts to infiltrate will be handled swiftly and severely."

"As if God would accept such temerity," Elija scoffed.

"Those galaxies, much like this one, evolved without shepherds or choirs to guide them. As such, they consider themselves independent and refuse to provide

succor or get involved in the eternal Heaven and Hell conflict."

"They wouldn't have a choice if Hell chose to invade," he scoffed.

"Hell has tried. And failed. As has Heaven."

Elija blinked. "What? How?"

"Because God and the Hell princes are powerful but they do have weaknesses. They can be hurt, damaged, even killed."

"Blasphemy." Elija huffed.

"Only blasphemy because God has declared it so. He isn't all-seeing, all-knowing, or all-powerful."

"God can perform miracles."

"He can, within a certain limit. As I recall, you once prayed to God to save a planet from impending doom, only to be ignored."

The reminder still stung. Elija ducked his head. "I was wrong to ask. And even more wrong to disobey his command." He and all the other angels in the choir had tried to forestall an impending disaster on a flock planet.

Against God's orders.

They'd been told to leave the vibrant colony to its fate, but the choir instead chose to help them survive the coming magnetic storms that would wipe the surface of life. To that end, they were guiding the flock as they created a shelter underground that would harbor them until the catastrophe passed.

Elija had been aboard the cantorii, getting patched by a Jesus after a severe burn when disaster struck.

The geomagnetic storms hit much, much earlier than expected. So early that his brothers on the surface all perished. Along with the flock.

All because they'd not listened to God. If they'd departed as told...

"*You weren't wrong in showing compassion to the colony. Helping them was the right thing to do. What you don't know was Elyon knew of your choir's actions and became angry. He viewed it as defiance that needed a lesson, hence why he had his scion trigger the holy fire which started the chain reaction to wipe the planet earlier than planned.*"

Elija stopped breathing. "*No.*" *The only syllable he could manage.*

"*Oh yes. You see, there was nothing wrong with that planet other than the fact the flock had begun to evolve and question the religion forced upon them. So Elyon did what he always does when he feels he's losing control of a flock. He gathers all the suul he can and wipes the surface clean to start over.*"

"*But my choir...*" *He couldn't say it. They'd been on the surface, helping to build shelter and moving supplies. None of it ready when the magnetic storms hit and shredded everything in its path.*

Metatron's expression turned bleak. "*Were used to set an example to others. It's only pure luck you survived. If the Atlantis hadn't taken care of the Jesus we travelled with, you could have asked him about it, seeing as he's the one who reported your choir's actions and triggered the Holy Fire."*

"He killed them."

"He did because they were expendable. As are we. Why do you think we were sent on such a long voyage into what should have been the unknown? You, me, and the others on that ship are Elyon's undesirables. We question. We've seen and experienced things."

"Leox is a true believer."

"Leox wants to be one, but he is struggling with his faith. We all are."

Elija wanted to call him a liar. He knew what he believed. Only, that wasn't true. Not anymore. He didn't understand God's plan in this instance. A plan that wanted them to intentionally destroy Eden with no attempt at salvaging anything.

"If you feel that way, then why have you been with him the longest?"

Metatron's expression pinched. *"In the beginning, I believed the choirs and shepherds were doing good. And in many cases, we are. But I've come to realize that one set of rules doesn't always work in the case where populations have expanded their consciousness past the gather-food-and-survival stage. The humans are a good example of what happens when minds are allowed to progress and think for themselves. They look at things from many perspectives. They allow for differences. For individuality of thought."*

"You make them sound almost better than angels."

"Who's to say they aren't?" Metatron fixed him with a sorrowful gaze. "What makes us superior to them?"

Elija could have listed petty reasons. Their longevity—only because of God's and his scions' healing. Their wings—again given to them by God. Their morals—again abiding by God's standards. His mind whirled as he realized just how little he actually controlled himself.

"I am but a puppet for his command." He didn't realize he'd spoken aloud until Metatron replied.

"And that is why you're on this voyage, because you'd already begun to think for yourself once before. Elyon knew it was only a matter of time before it happened again."

"I take it the scion came along to spy for him," his sarcastic reply.

"No, he also was considered unfit. You see that particular Jesus Christ had a bit of a killing problem, as in the choirs he worked with had a tendency to die."

"Like the one I served with." Jesus had intentionally murdered his brothers. "How did he become bad?"

"Because even God can't control everything. Every now and then, his flock strays."

Elija closed his eyes. "So he sent a killer with our choir, knowing he'd eventually betray us."

"Luckily, I was aware of his predilection. I had him prohibited from accessing Heaven's flame on the cantorii."

"But not the transporter or communication system."

Metatron turned his lips down. "I misjudged just

how depraved he could be. The Atlantis did us a favor."

"You didn't want to deal with Jesus."

"Would you? And now that we've cleared that up, on to the reason why I requested to see you. It concerns the seed mission."

"Are you canceling it?"

"No. But I will make it easier." Metatron reached for a box on the table, flipping back the lid and removing from it a smooth and rounded rock, which he thumped down. "This will take care of the transportation of the seeds. You just need to bring it into their vicinity."

Elija eyed the stone. "What does it do?"

At his query, Metatron smiled and said the most unangelic thing. "Magic." He then added, "Anything in direct line of sight of the baetylus can be beamed. Including you, should you run into trouble."

The stone now rested in a pouch at Elija's hip, inside his pants. Secure until they needed it.

He loaded up a journey sack with as many items as he dared. Last, he grabbed the mirror, a polished metal with a handle on the back much like a shield. Only this one could pulverize anything reflected on its surface at a distance of two paces or less. Any further and its power fizzled.

He hefted it onto his shoulder and glanced around. Should he take anything else?

His gaze went to a divinii dagger hanging on the wall, one of a few weapons on board not keyed to a single angel. Would it work for a human? Would the petite Lulu be able to use it against something of flesh and blood? Only one way to find out.

He tucked it into his belt before heading back to his room. Only Munna remained inside.

Elija frowned. "Where's Cindy-lu?"

"Gone."

"What do you mean gone?" He blinked at his brother. "Gone where?"

Munna rolled his eyes. "To the surface of course. Something about wasting daylight while you moped."

"I was not moping," he huffed hotly.

"Whatever. She asked the cantorii for what she needed. Once she'd outfitted herself, she left."

"You should have waited before you beamed her." Elija couldn't help his annoyance. She'd gone ahead, alone, without a proper weapon—or a goodbye.

"Don't blame me. I told her to wait for you, but she said she needed to get there early to scout during daylight. And so she asked the cantorii, and poof, she was gone." Munna spread his hands. "Don't worry, I know where she went, and where you're supposed to meet up with her tonight." Munna went on to pull up a map with his HALO and point out where Cindy-lu planned to make camp for the night.

"Assuming she makes it there." Elija made a mental note of it, but remained concerned about the more immediate issue. He gnashed his teeth before saying aloud, "Show me Cindy-lu's location." The map in front of them didn't move. He growled. "I said show me where she is."

The cantorii obeyed, its sight resetting the map until it was just a speck of land surrounded by water, and then zeroing back in on it so it grew as the view zoomed closer. Soon he saw an airport, with its flying planes and ugly buildings the humans used as terminals. A few roads, surrounded it, not showing much movement. A cold white snow clung to the ground.

"I don't see her," he stated.

The cantorii zeroed in on a few heads exiting a terminal, one of them wearing a bright pink hat with a fuzzy ball on the end. The person wore a puffy gray jacket, big glasses against the glare coming from the snow, and carried a bag.

It had to be Cindy-lu. Strutting with confidence. Intent on completing her mission.

Past her, a few paces away, leaning against a vehicle marked Taxi, a familiar face.

"It's the Hell Prince," he exclaimed as he recognized Astaroth from images he'd seen.

The moment the realization hit, the image abruptly cut off and Munna exclaimed, "We're being blocked from seeing."

More important, though, Cindy-lu was all alone and in grave danger.

CHAPTER 9

I saw him as I exited the airport. Mr. A himself. My ex-boss—and demonic Hell prince stuck on Earth—casually leaned against a taxi as if he waited for me.

So much for trying to cover our tracks.

Avoiding him seemed kind of pointless. Surely he wouldn't do anything in such a public place.

I headed for Astaroth, conscious I lacked a decent weapon. The cantorii could provide a bunch of stuff, but it had no concept of combustion or gunpowder. It offered me a baton for whacking instead. Would Mr. A stand still while I beat him into unconsciousness?

I stopped a pace away and threw myself into the confrontation. "Are you here to finally pay what you owe me? I'm still missing my last few paychecks and severance."

He smiled at me, a wide toothy grin that

belonged on a crocodile. The angels called him a Hell prince. Supposedly part demon. I saw him more as a monster, one who'd intentionally called Hell knowing it would destroy the planet.

"Sue me," was his reply for gross employee negligence.

"I've got better things to do."

"Ah yes, such as loading up the Atlantis for its voyage."

I pinched my lips. "Surely you can't mind if a few people and supplies manage to escape. Just think, maybe they can settle another planet that you can eventually pillage."

"Settled by the pure of heart, I'm sure." He rolled his eyes as he pushed away from the car. "Of which you won't be one. None of my former Novae staff will be in the chosen group, I'd wager seeing as how you all worked for a big bad evil Hell prince."

"Nothing's been decided yet."

"It has. And you're not so stupid as to not see it."

I knew I wouldn't make the cut, but I'd honestly kind of hoped I'd be one of those last-minute, "Hey, we need to have Cindy-lu," picks to go. "All that matters is that our species survives."

"Throwing in the towel already," he taunted.

"Did you come all this way just to be a prick?" I countered.

"I came to ask you to join me. Unlike Heaven's choir, we appreciate people of all ages and experiences. Your ability to think would be celebrated on Hell."

"Are you seriously inviting me to the dark side?" I gaped at him. And then, being a smartass, added, "Do you have cookies? And not the cheap kind. I am talking about the oh-my-god, these-cookies-are-so-moist-and-delicious version."

"We have everything a heart can desire."

"And what if I want my planet to not be raped of everything?"

"That I cannot give you. Although it might recover. Eventually. I imagine it will take centuries before Earth restores itself from the mining of its resources. If it doesn't fracture. There are some pockets of interest under its crust."

"You're assuming we won't stop the invasion." I lifted my chin.

He smirked. "I know you won't because I've lived here long enough to know there is no way all the countries in the world will agree and work together in unison."

"They did it before, during the pandemic."

"And we all saw how that turned out. Still protests and arguments about it today. Imagine how the world will react when it realizes its doom is imminent. People will bargain anything to live. Hell will have to turn away applicants for its fighting arenas and worker pool. Those not chosen will die a gruesome death as Hell strips everything that helps them survive."

"Humanity won't let evil win." I truly believed it.

And for a second, I saw uncertainty in Astaroth's gaze, quickly replaced by a confident smirk. "Maybe you aren't as smart as I thought. But the offer still stands. Think about it." He winked before he disappeared from sight, and if I'd not recently seen the same thing, I might have been more impressed.

Astaroth possessed a cloak of hiding. Not good. It meant he could sneak up at any time with no one the wiser.

"Where did the Hell prince go?" I recognized the voice as Elija's, and yet I jumped and squeaked, seeing as he spoke from the empty spot beside me.

People eyed me oddly, and I smiled weakly. "The air is so cold." People shook their heads in bemusement at my strange mannerisms. I sidled away from them before whispering, "What are you doing here?"

"Upon checking on your status, I saw the Hell prince."

"Spying on me?" I huffed.

"You left," his disembodied voice countered.

"Because that was part of the plan."

"I don't like your plan." He couldn't have sounded more petulant if he tried.

"I don't care." I harangued while also being relieved. I remained unsure of Astaroth's intentions.

Surely he'd not tracked me down merely to offer me a job in Hell?

"The Hell princes are tricky."

"I know. I've dealt with one in case you've forgotten," I muttered as I reached the end of the cleared area with nothing left of interest.

"What did he want?"

"Me."

For a second, an angry face appeared from within the folds of the cloak. I really hoped nobody noticed the floating, bodiless visage.

"Someone will see you," I hissed. He tucked back away, and I said quickly, "He came here to see if he could lure me to his side."

"And?"

"And what?"

"Did he lure you?"

"Wow, you really have no respect for me at all." I snorted. "Just to make it clear, *no*. He didn't lure me to his side." I stalked away from Elija, back to the single taxi remaining, not the one Astaroth had been leaning on. A peek inside showed a red-cheeked woman in a plaid buttoned shirt behind the steering wheel.

I tossed my bag inside before climbing in, knowing Elija had to be close but unable to do anything without showing himself. I slammed the door shut and leaned forward.

"I heard someone here can outfit me with

camping gear and a snowmobile. I wanna go somewhere I can see all the night lights in the sky."

"I wouldn't advise going alone. It's easy to get turned around." She spoke English with a heavy accent.

I smiled at her. "Don't worry about me. I never get lost." I'd always had an innate ability to find the right direction.

"All right then, I know just the person to help."

It took just over an hour to get geared up. The guy renting the snowmobile advised me of the tracker on the machine, which I could turn into an SOS if I got into trouble. It could also be used to find it should I not return in two days, the length of my rental. The sled came with a tag-along for my camping gear—a popup tent, a heavily insulated sleeping bag, water, food, a camp stove, and even a lithium-battery-powered heater.

"All the comforts of home," I'd joked as I paid for everything in cash and then used the identification the cantorii faked to sign my name as Mary-sue Mathews.

I'd not seen or sensed Elija since the airport. I wondered if he tried to follow me on foot. The car hadn't been moving all that fast. I really hated that a part of me hoped he was nearby.

My encounter with Astaroth had shaken me, even as I realized he could have easily abducted me had he wanted to. But instead, he'd just talked and then told me he'd be back for my final answer. When? Did I need to worry?

If I did start making myself anxious, I might chicken out on the mission. I couldn't now, not being so close.

I exited the equipment rental place to notice the sun already appeared to want to set way too early. That was fine. Early dark meant fewer people out and about in the actual evening when we'd start our climb and breaking in. It would also help Elija reach the rendezvous point sooner than later.

I straddled the snowmobile, wearing the slim-fitting snowsuit the cantorii fabricated. The tag-along sled was attached and its load covered in a tarp. The helmet went on and plugged into the machine, the visor heating to prevent fogging. Rather than listen to the burr of the engine, I chose to use the Bluetooth to play the only station on the island.

To the strains of a song I'd never heard, I set out, following the road out of the small town and then following the GPS, already programmed to lead me to the vault. There was no point in pretending I'd not come for it. Not now that Astaroth knew.

My nape prickled, and I couldn't help but look around a lot as I drove. My head craned left and right, up and back over my shoulder. My paranoia about imps had me hypersensitive.

Nothing in the sky. Nothing on my tail.

Still, I couldn't shake the jittery sense of being watched. I parked my ride in view of the mountain I'd have to hike. Hopefully Munna had told Elija where to meet me. He'd left rather abruptly. Then again, so had I.

In my defense, he'd questioned whether or not I'd turned traitor and joined Mr. A's team. And that was after he'd gone off in a snit about not liking my plan—not that he'd offered an alternative to consider. What did he want, for us to sit around on the cantorii forever, debating strategies while Hell moved closer and closer to Earth? Knowing he hadn't liked my idea to steal the seeds in the first place, I couldn't help but suspect he stalled so I'd figured the best move would be to go forward with the only plan we had.

In retrospect, that was a bad move on my part. I kept forgetting the enemy we dealt with wasn't an academic who'd crucify anything I published in a scathing rebuttal piece but a psycho who would kidnap, torture, and kill.

And somehow, he'd known where I'd be.

Good thing the cantorii gave me a club.

Ugh.

With the snowmobile parked, I removed my helmet and swapped it for a hat that tucked over my ears. I trudged to the sled, the tarp on it flatter than when I started. As I looked, the ties on it began unsnapping themselves. I stopped and stared. Ping.

Ping. One by one they came undone and the tarp tugged free.

"The ghost thing is not funny," I muttered. "Reveal yourself before I give you a whack." Yes, I raised my oh-so-menacing baton in the air.

Rather than remove the cloak, Elija said, "It's me," easing my concern it might be Astaroth.

"Elija? How did you get here before me? I thought you were supposed to wait for dark to fly." I glanced at the clear sky, starting to shift colors already. I'd better get moving or I'd be setting up the tent in the dark. It would be much too early to move it. At this time of day, the vault plateau might still be crawling with tourists. Not a ton, mind you, but even one person watching would be too much. We didn't need anyone interfering.

He continued to unload the sleigh as he explained, "I hitched a ride, first atop the roof of your conveyance then on your sled."

"Are you insane? That was so dangerous," I exclaimed, waving my hands, while really hoping nobody watched because I'd look like the crazy lady talking to thin air.

"I've ridden faster worms on the Waareeo desert planet," he scoffed.

"I meant you could have been seen, dumbass." God did not strike me down for calling his angel a name.

Elija went silent and stopped moving.

"Hello? Well, did anyone see you?"

"I don't believe so. I kept the cloak wrapped tight."

A heavy sigh slipped from me. "it's not like it really matters. Astaroth knows we're here. He could be a foot from me, and I'd never know." I glanced left as if searching.

"That's an unexpected development," he admitted.

"How did he get one of those cloaks?"

"I don't know. Perhaps it was stolen from the choir that came before us."

"Or maybe it's not just God who can make magical toys."

Apparently my words were a catalyst, because the hood went back, leaving him a bobbing head with a rounded mouth. "You can't be seriously hinting that Hell can bless items like Elyon."

"Why not? Can you state with one hundred percent certainty that only your God can make magical relics?"

His mouth opened and closed then remained dropped as he stared at me with a glazed expression, almost pained, as if he'd been struck with my club. A glance down showed it still dangling by my thigh.

Apparently, my words hit him hard. "You okay?"

"Do you know I never once questioned his miracles?" He ducked his head. "I accepted many things, some that didn't make sense."

"It's easy to just be part of the crowd."

"And there's the not wanting to be punished." A wry grin twisted his lips. "We saw what happened to those who disobeyed Elyon. I lost almost an entire choir because we chose to ignore his command."

The pain in his eyes had me wondering if this incident was the one relived in his nightmares. "I'm sorry."

"So am I, because I spent too much time since blaming myself. And now here I am again, questioning my orders."

"What orders?"

He turned from me, a head with no body. I couldn't stand it. "Either put up your hood or take off the cloak because you are freaking me out," I snapped as I reached for the lantern. I had a pair. One oil, one electric with a solar charger for the meager amount of day we'd get to charge it. I lit the wick of the first and set it on a flat surface as I went after the package with the tent.

Fabric tickled past me, nothing I could see, only feel. The bottom of my sled disappeared. I glanced behind to see Elija shed the cloak. He stood there in all his winged glory.

"Dude! The light." I tried to shield him from its glare in case someone wondered about the strange shape he made. "I don't know if we're alone out here or not."

"I don't care if I'm seen."

"You say that now, but when a mob comes rampaging into our camp looking for an angel, don't blame me." I tugged out tent poles and sorted them by size.

"There is no one out here. And even if they did see, maybe it's time they started realizing we're real. It might make saving humanity easier."

Blame deep fakes and a suspicious public for assuming the angels were just a prank.

"And you just had to have this revelation now, only hours away from breaking into the biggest seed vault in the world?"

"Is there ever a good time?" he asked with a roll of his shoulders.

He had a point.

"Help me set up our tent because, despite your epiphany, we are not moving up the timeline. While you're ready to come out of the spaceship and say hello to the world, my priority is those seeds. We'll hit the mountain after midnight as planned. By then, all the tourists should be in their beds or sleeping bags."

"That is quite a bit of time for you to be exposed to the elements." He frowned. "Perhaps if you get in the sled, I can cover you for warmth while keeping watch."

"Or we could put this tent together and look like normal campers."

"What is a tent?"

There was something comical in watching a big capable angel muttering under his breath in his melodic language as I tried to teach him the joys of poles being threaded into canvas and them pulling the whole thing taut, the canvas tubes attached to clear plastic sections that offered a panoramic view from inside the globe.

He grimaced. "Our shelter is a bubble?"

"Great visibility from all directions, and it will help keep the heat in. Give me a second to grab and toss a few things inside." I spread out the sleeping bag first, with its built-in inflatable layer to provide some insulation against the ground. The refillable gas canister that fit in my palm did wonders inflating the thin mattress. I unzipped and folded a corner back, my ass in the air when he entered the dome behind me.

Suddenly my spacious snow globe felt very tight.

He was so big.

So very very big.

I whirled as a shiver of desire went through me. Camping on a frozen tundra before a save-the-world event was not the right time to be having those thoughts.

"I need to get something from the sleigh." I squeezed past him without waiting for a reply, the frigid air kissing my fiery cheeks. I pulled my knapsack free with its rations and the portable electric heater. I loved new technology. There was a time I'd have had to burn a dirty fire for warmth.

It required no ventilation, so we could sit right inside the tent. A tent Elija had taken over. He'd made himself comfortable sitting cross-legged, his wings wrapping around the curve of the dome, leaving little room for me.

I set the heater down beside the exit and got it going, the blower humming right away and pushing hot air.

I sat with my back to it, the only spot available unless I crawled into that tempting lap. The man wore leather pants. Or so they seemed. They molded his legs and had a malleability that allowed him to sit with his legs fully bent. He'd matched it with a shirt that wrapped around his waist and then snapped in the front with a collar that did the same. He'd not worn a jacket. Must be nice.

I got hot inside my coat and unzipped.

"This is an interesting design," he commented, glancing around. "A little small, but a modified version would do very well in some places I've visited."

"Oh, like where?" I asked, shedding my coat, only to still sweat with the hot air blasting from the heater at my back.

"Not places you would have heard of."

"Places... as in more than one? Are there many planets like Earth out there?"

He glanced at me. "I've never encountered a place quite like Earth, but yes, there are many flocks and colonized planets. It is the only way to ensure Heaven never runs out of suul, given how Hell likes to steal."

"And these other flocks..." I almost grimaced to use his term. "Do they look like us? Two arms and legs, faces, speech?"

He nodded. "Mostly. Manipulation of genetics ensures the flocks are similar physically, with the variations coming from planetary adaptation."

"What about plants? Does your God also play with vegetation, or is it just people he likes to mess with?"

"Sometimes a planet will be found that has the potential for growth. The arks are equipped with the tools needed to make them into livable habitats."

"Do the arks create stuff out of astrayla like the cantorii?" I said create, and yet since I didn't know the science behind it couldn't help but think of it as magic. Like a genie granting wishes.

"Yes, to a certain extent. It can't make something it's never learned about."

"Learn how?"

He frowned. "I'm not sure. It's not something they covered in my lessons."

I couldn't help but wonder if the cantorii and arks got their knowledge from people's heads. The way it had fed me some of my favorites without asking, conjured up clothes in the exact style and material I would have chosen for myself...

"Why is it the arks use astrayla but your God needs suul?""

"I don't know. Do you always ask so many questions?"

My turn to offer a shrug. "I'm curious. Aren't you?"

His mouth opened and shut, nothing coming out for a moment until he finally said, "I didn't used to be."

"Hang around me for a while and you'll soon be wondering about everything." I shifted, as my ass felt as if it burned.

"You are uncomfortable."

"Just hot because the heater is too close to my back."

Before I could even think to protest, he'd dragged me into his lap, my back to his chest. It provided a different kind of heat. The kind that brought a blush to my cheeks. To hide my reaction, I shoved at my glasses even though they remained firmly on my nose.

"Better?" he murmured against me.

"Yeah." The problem being it reminded me of the kiss, which didn't help the arousal coursing through my veins.

"You appear tense."

"Most men ask permission before putting a

woman in their lap." I alluded to part of my discomfort. Although it should be known I liked being in his lap. He'd just taken me by surprise.

"Would you like to sit in my lap?"

I knew he didn't say it to be dirty, but my mind... Boy, did it have ideas that involved fewer clothes.

"Let me know if I get too heavy," was my lame reply.

A quiet settled around us, along with the last of twilight. The stars overhead appeared with a vividness I never got to see in the city. I wondered if we'd get any of the colored light shows famous in this part of the world.

"I had an interesting conversation with Metatron today," he said out of the blue.

"About?"

"If I were to condense it into the simplest terms, duty, and conscience."

"I know you're all about duty." His earlier rejection made that clear.

"I wasn't always," he admitted. "There was a moment where I questioned. Where I didn't do my duty. I went against God's command and tried to save people that he wanted gone."

"What happened?" I asked, dreading the answer.

"Except for me and Jesus, everyone died. At the time, I blamed myself for defying Elyon. He'd told us to leave. We chose to stay and help. I lived with that guilt and swore I'd never disobey again."

"What happened to change that?"

"You. This planet. Another impossible order."

I tensed. "Wait, are you saying..." I trailed off.

He muttered softly. "Elyon wants us to leave and to take nothing with us."

"He wants Hell to kill us?"

He said nothing for a moment. "It's worse. He wants us to destroy your moon."

"But that would completely mess up the Earth." He said nothing, and I uttered an, "Oh." Then a deeper, "oh," of understanding.

"He wants us to destroy Earth, just like he destroyed Doraado and my brothers."

"And you're having an epiphany of faith? Over what? He's a psychopath."

"I am Elyon's Warrior. I'm supposed to obey my God."

There are many things I could have said, but what emerged from my mouth? The truth. "Are you sure he's the good guy? What makes him different than Astaroth or any of the Hell princes?"

"I don't know," his quiet admission. "But I am no longer prepared to simply follow. And if he smites me, so be it. I will help you and the other humans because it is the proper thing to do."

"Thank you. And I have to say I'm impressed you

changed your mind and told me about it. Most guys would have never said a thing."

"Think of it as a very long-winded apology. I am sorry for my attitude in your regard. It was not deserved. You are a fierce and intelligent being who deserves my respect and a weapon."

"Er... what?" His lovely speech ended so oddly it left me at a loss for words. My intelligence lowered a few more notches as he shifted underneath me, his groin and hips rotating against me in a way that made me think of sinful things that would have made my poor angel blush.

"I have something for you," he said in that deep rumbly voice of his.

Judging by the bulge under my bottom, he sure did.

"Here. Put your hand around it and tell me what you think."

I'd love to wrap my hand—

My jaw dropped as he pressed warm metal into my palm.

A dagger, not a dick.

I'd have been more disappointed if I'd not noticed the sheen hueing the blade. "Is that divinii?"

"Yes. Not as strong a dose as that imbuing my sword, but it will do more damage than one of your Earth knives."

I turned it in my hand to admire it, the fine

tooling on the hilt. The way it felt light in my grip, but sturdy. "Does Heaven have blacksmiths?"

"All weapons are provided by Elyon."

"Where does he get the designs?"

"I don't understand."

I pointed to the intricate twining of thorned vine and leaf. "This is lovely. Ethereal. The strokes of it are light and feathery. Very delicate. But your sword, on the other hand…" I patted the sheath running the length of his leg. "It's got deep bold etches. A much different style. As if by another hand."

"You don't think God created the weapons?"

"I think it's more likely that he acquired them and spelled them with his magic, or if created by whatever method he uses, the original design was taken from someone else, most likely in the same way the cantorii reads my mind and conjures things."

"Why does it matter?"

"Don't you want to know?" I countered.

"There is only one thing I'm thinking about right now."

"What is that?"

"Did you like kissing me?" The question emerged firm, and yet I sensed the trepidation behind it.

The courage to even ask.

"Oh yes." I didn't even try to hide my reaction. "I am also very much enjoying sitting in your lap."

"I like it as well."

I half turned so I could see his face. "Are you always this awkward when you flirt?"

"I've never flirted."

"I can see why. Does this mean you're a virgin?"

"N-n-no," he stammered in embarrassment. "But you're nothing like those I've been with."

"Comparing me to them?" I teased.

"There is no comparison," he muttered.

I reached up to stroke his jawline. "You just keep surprising me."

"Is that a good thing?"

"How do you feel when I surprise you?"

He offered a wry grin. "My heart stops. And then it beats too fast."

I'd never heard a nicer thing. I leaned in close and kissed him. His mouth clung to mine, teasing and coaxing my lips to part.

We embraced sweetly at first, soft, with gentle motions, but my blood soon boiled, demanding more. I pressed my mouth harder against his. My hands fisted his shirt before tugging it upward to palm the ridged muscles of his stomach. Without a belly button, I noticed. A question for another day.

He turned fierce with his embrace, his tongue being the first to venture for a slide. I shivered in his arms. As we continued to kiss, I turned in his lap to straddle him, our clothes preventing the friction of bare flesh and exciting nonetheless. I rubbed and ground myself against him. He palmed my ass. He kissed me so hard and long and deep I felt tingles in my pussy.

When he unsnapped my pants and made it past my long johns into my panties, I leaned back to give him better access and panted. He cupped me, his hand warm against my moist and needy flesh. His touch, hesitant at first as he traced me, teasing the opening of my sex, outlining my nether lips, drawing a gasp when he explored my clitoris.

I held on to his shoulders as his hand grew bolder in its movements, his thumb stroking my nub while his fingers penetrated.

I had to lean forward and kiss him as I rode his hand. My breath fast and harsh. His equally ragged. Our foreheads touched, and it was like I'd entered a dream.

An erotic one because, suddenly, it wasn't his fingers thrusting in and out of me but his cock. As if caught in a mirage, I clung to him as he pounded me. I couldn't hold on to the pleasure. I came, hard and fast, and kind of loudly, which he thankfully caught with his mouth.

My body shuddered, my pussy twitched and convulsed.

His lips moved against mine as he murmured, "Why is everything with you so much better?"

Before I could explain how I was just so epic and that. really, the world revolved around me, a shadow passed overhead, blotting out the starlight.

I glanced up just as more shapes blocked the stars overhead.

While I cursed, Elija growled, "Imps."

CHAPTER 10

ELIJA COULD HAVE BANGED HIS HEAD ON THE GROUND IN frustration. Because while he'd been busy thinking about his wants, his needs, his pleasure—and being utterly selfish—imps had not only approached but gone past them.

Lulu reacted more quickly than him. She grabbed her clothing and dove out of the tent shouting, "They're heading for the vault."

Of course they were because, unlike them, the imps didn't care if they were seen.

It took some ungainly maneuvering to exit the dome. He emerged to see her snaring her bag and running for the mountain, jacket flapping since she'd not tied it. He eyed his own sack and the mirror, the one heavy, the other unwieldy. If he took those, he couldn't fly with her. He left them on the ground and ran for her instead and scooped her mid-step before leaping into the air.

"What are you doing?" she yelled.

"Taking you to the top."

"Put me down. You need to bring the relics. We're going to need them."

She had a point. He set her back on her feet, and she continued to sprint while he banked and dipped around to grab his supplies. The mirror went over his forearm, the sack strapped heavily at his hip, opposite his sheath. He hadn't yet pulled his sword, and he flexed those fingers, wondering. Maybe she wouldn't be too much weight.

As if she read his mind, she yelled, "You'd better get there before those imps wreck anything! Throw a sleep bomb. Slow them down."

He pinched his lips tight. He understood duty. He arrowed for the top of the mountain, his wings pumping hard and making up for the time lost since the imps had passed by. He crested in time to spot the imps alighting before a ramp leading to a tall rectangular structure built into the mountain. The group of imps hesitated to cross it.

The reason? Munna stood there with his spiked hammer, waiting. The other angel saw Elija coming and grinned. "About time you showed up."

"Lulu is at the bottom of the mountain," he murmured as he slipped behind his brother, dropping the sack on the ground.

"Then go get her! I can handle this crew!" The still wounded Munna didn't let the fact he fought on two feet stop him. He tapped the haft of his hammer in his palm and bellowed, "Which of you ugly critters wants to be first?"

The imps scattered as Munna charged off the ramp. Elija slid the mirror to lie atop the bag of relics before leaping into the air and arrowing back down the mountain.

Just in time!

A huffing Cindy-lu, wearing a light that shone from her hat, waved the dagger he'd given her at a hissing creature the likes of which he'd never seen. It reminded him of a demon with its horns and glowing eyes, but the rest of it appeared as an animal. It walked on four paws, its squat body covered in brindled white and gray fur.

She yelled as she stabbed wildly in its direction. No finesse or skill, just a lot of menacing enthusiasm, which kept the beast at bay. He drew his sword in a smooth motion that kept it on its arcing path as he landed between Cindy-lu and the threat.

The head went tumbling, and the body fell over, its steaming blood staining the snow.

She squeaked, "What the fuck was that?"

"The reason why I shouldn't have left you alone," he growled. From much too close, he heard snarls and growls. While he couldn't see them yet, he sensed three, possibly more, creatures racing in their direction. "We have to go."

He swept her into his non-sword-bearing arm, wrapping it around her waist and tucking her to his chest. She wisely wrapped her arms around his neck and her legs around his hips.

"You are supposed to be fighting imps," she complained as he leaped into the sky and began flapping. Just in time, as a furry body leaped through the spot where they'd been standing.

"Munna is handling them. And a good thing. Had I not returned, that might not have ended well."

"I would have been fine if someone would just give me a gun," she grumbled. "What is it with you all wanting me to fight close enough I can feel their breath on my face?"

"That is the way—"

She interrupted. "Don't you pull some mystical Mandalorian shit on me."

"What is a Mandalorian?"

"Not the point. I can't win in a hand-to-hand fight. A gun increases my odds of survival."

"What of honor?" he asked as they neared the edge of the mountain.

"Survival trumps honor, especially in war. Sometimes you have to do ugly things for the greater good."

"Now you sound like Elyon."

"The difference being *his* good and *my* good aren't the same thing. It's all a matter of the side you're on," she said as he angled over the plateau in front of the building. He'd been taking in an aerial view while listening to her.

What struck him most was the comment about survival. It reminded him of Zakai, his somber brother who'd been a prisoner of Dante's Inferno, where he'd endured much suffering to survive. It would have been easy for him to give up and die, but he'd chosen to live and done things that required him to ask forgiveness of Elyon in front of his peers.

"Forgive me, Father, for I have sinned." Elija still remembered Zakai's frail form as he knelt before God. Not the real God but a projection of him in their barracks.

Elyon put a cone of silence around Zakai as he confessed so no one heard exactly why Zakai prayed to God. Elija still didn't know. However, he'd not been the only one to hear Elija's screams at night at the beginning of their voyage.

As he descended to the ground, he noted Munna standing triumphant amidst the five imp bodies he'd piled by the ramp. He'd managed to handle all of them and left none for Elija.

Elija sheathed his sword as he alit and set Cindy-lu on her feet.

She immediately went to the other angel,

exclaiming, "What are you doing here? You're supposed to be taking it easy with that wing."

Munna grinned. "As if I could resist. Elija went tearing off the moment he saw the Hell prince. I tried to remove the block preventing us from seeing, but once I realized I couldn't, I had the cantorii beam me down discreetly. Almost had an incident with a human, as I transported in blind. Once I realized no one crossed the ramp, I waited, knowing you'd arrive once it got dark."

All excellent planning, and yet Elija wanted to snarl when Cindy-lu patted him on the arm and praised him. "I'm glad you came. Those imps could have caused so much trouble."

"Not really," Elija countered as he frowned at the five bodies. "Astaroth didn't send many."

"Which is surprising," Lulu said, finishing his thought. "You'd think with Astaroth being in the area, he'd have more of his minions."

"These were scouts," Munna said, his attention directed to a spot behind Elija.

Elija whirled to see a cloud approaching, its very mass blotting out the stars in the sky.

"Please tell me those are birds," Lulu whispered.

"I can't lie," Elija replied.

"This isn't good," Munna remarked on the obvious. "How long will it take you to get those seeds?"

Lulu glanced at him. "I don't know. The thing

Metatron gave you to help with the removal of the seeds? You have it?"

Elija patted his hip. "Right here, but it will only work in sight of the items we wish to transport."

"Well then, what are you waiting for?" She pointed to the mirror. "Blast open that door."

"First, let's make sure we give ourselves time." He dropped to his knees to dig his hand into the bag. He distributed the antidote first, and then, as Munna and Cindy-lu drank it, he began pulling out the sleepy spheres.

As Lulu handed back the antidote, he took a dose before snaring the mirror.

"Put them to sleep while I get the vault open." He held up the relic and gave a little prayer in Heaven's language, "What can be seen, now be undone. Dash it to pieces then ground into dust." He didn't know if it needed the prayer to work, but the grip warmed in his hand, even as the mirror didn't emit any light or make a sound. Everything reflected in its surface, in this case the vault door at less than a pace, ceased to exist, as did all air molecules. The dead space didn't last long, as more atmosphere rushed in, the sudden movement of air stirring the fine silt left behind.

He now had a small opening, which might fit Cindy-lu if she squeezed. He repeated the prayer as he rotated his arm to widen the hole.

Puff. The space widened. On his fourth prayer to

finish off the opening so he could fit without scraping his wings, Munna stated, "They're here."

The leathery whip of wings filled the air, and Elija flipped around to see a dark night turn even more ominous as the horde of imps covered the sky in a sea of writhing evil.

As if controlled by one mind—and just maybe they were—they landed, hundreds of them, including some demons, their horns ranging from stubby to curved. They filled the space on the other side of the small ramp. An undulating wave of menace.

More than they could fight.

"Put them to sleep." Elija dropped the mirror and grabbed a large sphere.

Munna hefted another. Cindy-lu, on the other hand, grabbed a small one and dashed it at her own. The air sparkled as the sleepy potion hung while it waited for a victim.

They remained immune, and before he could ask why, she muttered, "Now no one can sneak up on us."

Smart.

Munna lobbed his into the crowd. The sphere got snatched midair and carried off.

Unexpected.

Elija tossed his next, aiming for the ground before them. His sphere shattered, but the ranks of demons and imps had rapidly shifted back, again as if under control, moving swiftly enough that only a few succumbed to the sleeping spell.

Too few.

A literal horde still faced them. Impossible odds. He flicked on his HALO. "Cantorii, beam us aboard."

"What? We can't," Munna protested.

As his brother got swallowed by a bright light, Elija replied, "I'm calling a retreat."

Being the one who ordered a withdrawal meant, under protocol, he'd go last to ensure everyone else got taken care of first. He waited for Cindy-lu to go next. She stood in the middle of the ramp, facing the army of darkness.

No light enveloped her.

He could feel his HALO activate. Had it misunderstood his order? Or assume he only meant angels? *"Evacuate Cindy-lu to the cantorii."* He made his command more precise, and nothing happened. Had the cantorii been compromised?

"Munna?" He tried contacting his brother next. Dead silence.

"They can't answer right now," Cindy-lu softly stated, still facing forward. "Zilla's being blocked."

"What? Who's Zilla?" he queried as he pulled his sword and thought how best to handle the threat. He still had a few sleeping bombs. If he could corral his enemy so they came at him only a few at a time, maybe he wouldn't be overrun.

"Zilla is the name the cantorii told me she liked,"

Cindy-lu answered. "Apparently, in studying some of Earth's lore, more specifically the Bible, she took on one of the mentioned names as her own. It's of Hebrew origin and means shadow. Apparently, she finds it fitting."

"She?" Since when did a cantorii choose a name and a gender? The elevation of cantorii to ark was usually something decided upon by God and involved a ceremony.

"We can talk about it later. We're about to have company."

The rank of imps and demons parted to let a tall fellow with slick dark hair pass. He wore a suit and nothing else that would keep him warm. He approached with long strides, a demon of the worse kind because he could hide in plain sight with his human features.

Despite Astaroth's banal exterior, the danger had never been greater.

Elija wanted to jump in front of Cindy-lu to offer his body as a shield. She might stab him if he did. Her fingers curled around the hilt of the dagger hidden under her coat. To the casual observer, she'd appear to be warming her hands. Having seen her in action with it, he didn't hold much hope she'd do much damage to the demon prince.

Astaroth stopped a few paces from the ramp and smiled. The flames in his eyes ignited as he offered a mocking, "Greetings, Elyon's Warrior. You must be Elija. I've heard so much about you."

"Leave now and you won't perish today." Elija didn't exactly lie. He intended to kill the demon prince if he could. If he failed, then he'd have kept his word.

"Are we going to start with the threats already? Not very nice, especially since I didn't come to converse with you." The demon prince turned his smile on Cindy-lu. "We meet again."

"You didn't waste any time following me. What do you want?" She didn't give any semblance of quarter or nicety.

"Playing coy, I see. Did you not tell the angel about my offer?"

"She has no interest in you or Hell." Elija couldn't help but reply.

The demon prince arched a brow. "Look at you, speaking for Cindy-lu. And here I took her for someone capable of answering herself."

"He's only repeating what I've told him. My answer is no," she stated firmly. "So go away and take your flying pet monkeys with you."

The mini horde stirred at the insult.

"Are you sure? Has your angel explained what you're giving up? Hell isn't the hellfire place seen in the Bible but a place where pleasure and vice can be fed if you belong to the right circle."

She rolled her shoulders. "I've never been the partying and vice type."

"There is more than one kind of temptation. Hell isn't primitive like Heaven. We don't wait for a cantankerous God to sprinkle his blessing. We believe in science."

"Says the guy who was gleefully talking about stripping this planet to its core. Such a waste."

"Over time, regrowth might occur."

"Greedy bastard."

"No such thing on Hell," Astaroth mocked.

Elija listened to their discourse. This was the most he'd ever heard someone from Hell speak. Most times the only noise he heard them emit was a gurgle as they died.

"Wouldn't it be smarter to cultivate worlds with resources and trade with them?"

Astaroth waved a hand and sniffed. "More complicated you mean. Prices changing all the time. Upstarts thinking they can demand rank in exchange for raw goods. Not to mention, they only mete out a fraction at a time, less than what we usually need and, given the length of time between visits, it's much easier to take it all."

"That's barbaric."

"As compared to Heaven, I assume?"

"They don't pillage entire planets but rather cultivate them."

"For suul. And if those who emit the suul

become too uppity? Or start trying to overthrow their masters? Then wham." Astaroth clapped his hands hard enough Elija almost flinched. "Colony annihilated so a new one can take its place. Because God likes his peons obedient. His angels being his stupidest." The smirk was aimed right at Elija.

"I'm not the stupid one who got stranded on a planet for, how long?" Elija mocked.

Astaroth never lost his smile. "Have you told Cindy-lu yet that you're going to destroy Earth on Elyon's orders?"

Her shoulders stiffened. "As if I'd believe that. After all, as you can see, the angels are on our side."

"Ah yes, because their paltry few can prevail against my army." He swept a hand behind him. "Even if they could, you won't win. Hell can't be stopped. And forget escape. For you at least. God has already forbidden them from taking any humans with them. If they do, they'll die. Then again, if they stay, they'll also die. Join me and you can survive the inevitable."

"No." Such bravery in her one word.

Astaroth shrugged. "Pity to waste such a brilliant mind. But there are others who will be willing to take your place."

"Evil never wins." She sounded sure of herself, but Elija caught the tremor of fear.

"Says the girl who has no idea of the game being played. A game that's been going on for millennia.

And will continue long past the death of this planet. It will move to the next. And the next."

"If we're all just going to die, then might as well croak here trying to take out the source of the problem, as opposed to waiting for Hell to do it." She pulled the dagger from its sheath, gripping it tight, and yet it wobbled in her shaky fist.

"With that kind of spirit, maybe I will find a way to keep you alive. After all, a prince needs heirs now that he's returning to his birthright. The ones I had previously didn't work out."

"You won't touch her." Elija couldn't help the seething words. Rage and jealousy hit him swiftly and fiercely.

"Oh, I will touch and impregnate her. Maybe atop your dead body. Because you will die today, and that little talisman you carry"—Astaroth gestured to Elija's pocket, where he carried the baetylus from Metatron—"will give me your ship."

How did Astaroth know about it?

The demon prince showed his teeth as he cooed, "Did you really think I came here just to argue with Cindy-lu? I didn't need my legion for that."

A trap. This was a trap, and they'd walked into it. He couldn't let Astaroth get a hold of the stone. What if he could use it to steal the cantorii?

His HALO blazed as he once more attempted to command it, *"Take us both back to the ship."*

No reply.

The prince smiled. "Oops. Did I jam your signal? My bad." He then lifted his hand, a signal for the horde to flutter into the air, spoiling Elija's plan to fight them only a few at a time.

Since they couldn't beam aboard the cantorii, it left them only one option to delay the inevitable.

Shutting off his HALO so he'd stop being a shining beacon, he grabbed Cindy-lu around the waist and set her behind him, trusting the fog of sleep still present on the ground at his feet would give him a moment. "Here. Take the stone and run inside. Find a seed room to use it." He handed over the pouch and could only hope the cantorii would obey her use of it. Elija pulled his sword, hefted a sleep sphere, and prepared to fight.

But Cindy-lu had other plans. She bent and snagged the mirror he'd dropped before huffing, "Don't be an idiot. You can't prevail against that many. Get inside the vault." She tugged him into the building, shoving him away from her as she whirled, holding up the reflective surface, and aiming it at the human-built part of the structure.

He couldn't have said how she got it to work. He didn't think it would for anyone but an angel reciting the prayer.

Dust began to fall as the human-made doorway reverted to the basic building blocks of every galaxy and, in doing so, destabilized the areas around it, and them. The entire structure trembled. Shivered.

Groaned as metal and cement and more felt the stress of losing part of base.

She grabbed him by the hand and yelled, "Run."

He dropped a sphere before dashing after her into the vault—the structure carved into the very stone of the planet. Dust chased them as the entrance collapsed, trapping them inside.

CHAPTER 11

Well, this is just great. What should have been a somewhat simple extraction of seeds had turned into a deadly drama.

I found myself being hurried by Elija, who had his wing tucked around me as a shield as we moved away from the collapse. Even with him sheltering me, dust followed, and I tried to not breathe too deep or start coughing, because if I gave in to that tickle, I'd be too busy bent over trying to expel a lung to find our seeds.

In better news, my actions had bought us some time.

We didn't go far before hitting a door. My headlamp illuminated enough for us to see the icy surface and its latch. While I fumbled it, Elija glanced behind.

"Are they following?"

"Not yet." A grim reply as he lobbed the last of his spheres into the space we'd just left, an added sleepy layer of protection.

"Good, then let's get to work."

He blinked at me. "You mean find a way to escape?"

I frowned at him. "We already have one." I held up the pouch with the talisman inside.

"I don't know if the baetylus will work. The cantorii usually prefers some kind of open access, even if it's a crack, to the outside for beaming. Otherwise, there can be issues."

The word baetylus was one I'd heard before from Tamara, who'd used one to find the Atlantis. "Zilla seemed pretty confident about it working." The image she'd projected being of me placing the rock in front of a big jar of seeds and letting it do its thing. No mention of an open door.

"In that case, let's give it a try." He gestured to the pouch.

"I will once you open that door."

"Why? It doesn't go outside."

"To fetch some seeds, duh. The reason we're here."

"You still want to try and remove them?" Of course he couldn't help but inject some incredulity.

So I gave him some exaggeration back. "Duh."

Once more he glanced in the direction of the

blocked entrance. "They could break through at any moment."

"Then stop wasting time arguing."

Elija sighed as he wedged himself against the frigid door, which creaked and groaned in protest; however, it did slide open. By the light shining from my hat, I saw containers. "Yes." I hissed as I dropped to my knees and pulled out the talisman—an innocuous-looking grayish rock. If I dropped it into a pile, I'd be hard-pressed to fish it back out.

I placed it on the floor and waited. Tapped it. Nothing. "Okay, super rock, do your thing." I eyed it before asking, "Does it need a prayer?"

"When Metatron handed it over, he didn't mention—"

The ceiling overhead began to vibrate. I looked up to see a spot turning bright, the rock illuminating and getting lighter.

Before I could even begin to wonder what I saw, I'd been dragged against Elija, and a wing wrapped around me.

Smushed against his chest, I mumbled, "What's going on? Are we under attack?"

"The cantorii made its own conduit to us by directing a thin beam of Holy Light to penetrate until it finds its baetylus."

"Really? So cool."

A series of images and emotions hit me from Zilla as our communication suddenly resumed, a feeling of pleasure and a bit of puffing pride at having figured out how to help. Brilliant really. She'd given me the one thing she could always hone in on. A piece of herself.

"Take the seeds," I thought back.

The light in the room brightened, and when it extinguished, Elija exclaimed, "The boxes are gone."

"Awesome." I slipped out from under his wing, smiling. "One batch down."

"Why does that sound as if you're going to search for more?"

I glanced at him over my shoulder as I picked up the talisman. "I told you before we're grabbing as much as we can. Unlike you angels with your one-flavor juice, humans like variety. Now, onward, my big burly door-opener. To the next storage room."

"You are taking an unnecessary risk."

"Someone has to do it. Why not me?" I liked the idea of making a difference.

"You are extremely willing to put yourself in harm's way."

"Aren't angels?"

He rolled his shoulders. "We are not many and thus have to be judicious in how we confront danger."

"Well, humans have this thing about being heroes. Apparently, I'm not immune." I winked. "You should try it. You'd look great in tights."

"Not amusing," muttered with a glower as he

stalked to the next door. He might be grumpy about it, but he muscled without pause when we reached the next access point. We collected four more rounds of specimens before he said, "Why does it seem as if you are communicating with the cantorii?"

"Because I am. Aren't you?"

"No. I turned my HALO off to make it harder to locate us."

"You don't need a HALO to talk to Zilla."

"Yes you do," he argued. "The HALO is how we communicate with the vessel we're assigned."

"Are you sure about that? You didn't have your HALO active when you talked to Zilla in space."

"Because we don't need to when on board, as speaking aloud conveys our commands."

"Or maybe you never needed it at all. Have you ever tried to talk directly to Zilla when you're not inside her?"

"No." He rolled his shoulders as he said it. At least he'd moved away from telling me we should leave. He'd been skittish and spent more time watching behind us than ahead. Meanwhile, I doubted the imps would spend much time digging in this cold weather.

When confronting them outside, I'd seen a few of them shivering in the front ranks. They might be scary looking, but they felt the weather, unlike Elija. Must be nice.

The only reason my face hadn't gone numb was because the whole burning-a-hole-into-the-sandstone raised the temperature temporarily to pleasant. Not long enough to hurt the seeds, I hoped, seeing as how they were beamed away within seconds.

"You should try talking to her," said as we moved deeper inside.

"Why hasn't she spoken to me?" he countered.

To my surprise, I got a reply from the cantorii. "Zilla claims God blocked her ability to contact you. That the HALO only allows her to receive commands and only reply to direct inquiries."

"Why would he do that?"

More images and thoughts filtered to me as Zilla explained. "According to her, when she realized she'd attained sentience, she tried speaking with Elyon about moving her to ark status. She actually really has a keen interest in colonizing. But your God took issue with what he deemed her temerity in approaching him and sent her on this mission."

Elija halted his step to offer an incredulous, "Zilla is too small to be an ark."

"What's size have to do with it? I thought being an ark had to do with sentience."

"Which comes with age, which is indicated by general girth."

"Wait, so because she's skinny she can't advance? Maybe she's mature for her age. And I'd be more concerned about the fact your God made it so Zilla couldn't speak to its own crew. Lucky for her, us humans don't have that problem."

Elija rubbed his face. "This is a lot to take in."

"Don't worry. I'll be happy to explain what I've learned later." I patted his cheek. "First, let's finish up in this refrigerator." I pointed to the next door.

We'd already beamed thousands of samples, and I could only hope Zilla kept track of them so I could compare them against the vault's records. I should have probably memorized a map of the rooms and what they held. It might have helped me know where to go.

The door before us opened with the least trouble of all of them thus far. Most likely it had a recent deposit.

I stepped inside, only to immediately pause. The boxes in here were strewn all over. Seeds on the ground, scattered and mixed. This chamber lacked the chill of the others, not exactly warm but not freezing either and with a pungent aroma wafting.

"There is something in here," Elija's ominous warning as he stepped in front of me, sword at the ready.

"Then it's time for us to leave," I announced, crouching to put the talisman down. I knew to cover my eyes as Zilla did her thing. The hole took only seconds to form. Seconds too long, as I heard the scrape of talon on stone.

"Beam us," I yelled-thought to Zilla, only to then shout, *"Hold on."* Where had Elija gotten to?

He'd literally disappeared from sight. Fucking concealing cloak.

I could have left him. Zilla awaited my command. But I'd heard the term "leave no man behind" too many times in my life to be able to do that without regret. Not to mention, hadn't I implied not that long ago that humans were braver than angels since Elija claimed his kind usually retreated if the odds were bad?

He'd stayed. Surely he knew what he was doing. I didn't, but I didn't let that stop me. Hopefully I'd live to not regret that choice.

I scuffed the seeds on the floor and had an idea. I grabbed a handful and threw them as far from me as I could, the seeds scattering and plinking to the floor in a mini shower.

It brought the danger exploding from between the rows, an enormous creature that I couldn't see well given in my terror my light kept bouncing.

Earlier, on the mountain, I'd encountered a monster. I mean what else to call the furry red-eyed thing that wanted to eat me? Apparently, that had been the baby version.

Mama, with her pendulous teats, stomped into view, my shaking headlamp not improving the view of her slavering jaw, molten-red eyes, and the fetid stench that wafted from her.

ELIJA

Where was Elija?

The beast opened its jaw and roared.

I yelled right back. "I can't believe you ruined my specimens!" If I kept her focused on me, Elija could sneak up and do his thing with his sword.

My distraction didn't entirely work. The monster's head swung left and knocked into nothing and sent it flying. Legs poked out of the cloak as he landed hard. Before the monster could bite them off, I was throwing things at it. A cracked bin. Seeds. I suddenly remembered my dagger and held it out, the glint of the blade drawing the creature's malevolent gaze.

It huffed as it faced me, leaning down, ready to charge. I had nowhere to really run, but I wanted to as it stalked for me.

I shuffled back, the noise flaring the monster's nostrils. "That's it, keep your eyes on me," I muttered. I began to wonder if Elija had been knocked too hard when the beast squealed. It shook its head, and I could see the cut in its neck, which widened.

The monster dropped into a pool of its own blood and a smell to make me almost puke. I pulled my turtleneck over my mouth as Elija flipped back his invisible cloak.

"Took your time," I huffed, the shock setting in and making my hands tremble.

"I'd planned to draw it away from you," he grumbled.

"My hero," I teased with a smile.

Only he didn't reply in kind but looked past me.

I whirled to see a hand emerging from thin air, reaching for the talisman on the floor.

Astaroth! He'd snuck up on us with his concealing cloak.

I dove without thinking, my fingers wrapped around the hilt of a dagger, which I plunged into the hand lifting the talisman.

A shrill scream by Astaroth led to his digits flexing and dropping my stone, but I was committed to my act of violence. My leap ended with me falling, my blade tearing through muscle and bone while Astaroth shrieked.

I pounced on the talisman and tucked it to my chest before heaving myself in Elija's direction. As he wrapped an arm around me, a bright beam of light enveloped us, but not before I saw Astaroth's terrible visage, his forehead pulsing with fat veins, his eyes blazing with infernal fury.

His lips moved, and while I couldn't hear, I knew what he said. "This isn't over."

Not by a long shot.

CHAPTER 12

THE CANTORII BROUGHT THEM ABOARD, WITH CINDY-LU exclaiming, "Holy smokes that was close." She trembled head to toe but, despite that, kept the baetylus hugged tight to her chest.

Elija could have chastised her in that moment. He'd known principalities to go off on their choir for less. Had they left earlier, she wouldn't have been in danger.

However, that would be denigrating what she'd done. She'd managed to salvage a portion of seeds and she'd struck a blow at Astaroth, even if she didn't know it. A divinii blade caused grievous wounds that didn't heal without serious blessing.

An injured Hell prince would be a rabid and bitter one. Making him even more dangerous. They'd have to be extra vigilant.

"That was very courageous of you to confront Astaroth," he said in reply.

"Terrifying you mean." She tossed the baetylus onto the bed. "He almost got the talisman. If he'd arrived like seconds earlier while we dealt with that monster…" She shook her head before suddenly gaping at him. "Do you think Astaroth put that beast in there on purpose?"

"Most likely." And the diversion almost cost them. They'd nearly lost the baetylus, which might have compromised the cantorii and their only way out of this galaxy if things went badly—which seemed likely.

"Well, at least we didn't beam away empty-handed." She glanced around his room. "Guess the seeds wouldn't have been stored in here." She glanced at the ceiling. "Hey, Zilla, can you show where they are?"

Rather than reply, bright light beamed Cindy-lu away, and he was left blinking. "Where did you take her?" he shouted in a sudden panic. An image appeared of her in a room with compartments in the wall. Cindy-lu peeked in their viewing windows and appeared to be speaking, given her moving hands and lips.

Safe, but, of more interest, she truly did talk with the ship. Could what she'd told him be true? Was the cantorii sentient but blocked from speaking to them? And if so, could it be reversed?

His HALO pinged. He allowed the incoming message.

"About time you replied!" Munna exclaimed. "I've been worried. The cantorii wouldn't send me back and we were blocked from seeing what happened. Once visuals did resume, you were gone and the building collapsed."

"We survived. Even got some seeds."

"Without me," Munna grumbled. "Why did you send me away? I would have helped."

"It wasn't me. Did you know Cindy-lu can talk to the cantorii?"

"Everyone can when aboard the ship."

"I meant while on the planet?"

A pause then Munna blurted out, "How? She doesn't have a HALO."

"Right?" Elija huffed, feeling somewhat vindicated.

"That seems kind of odd," Munna muttered. "We've never been able to give direct commands unless our HALO is lit. Though, it would be useful in demonic situations if we didn't have to light a beacon to our location just to ask a question of our ship."

"Cindy-lu further claims the cantorii told her it had its ability to speak directly to us blocked by Elyon."

"Why?"

Why indeed? "I don't know. But we have more

important things to deal with. Astaroth is more dangerous than we suspected. Is anyone else aboard?"

"Just us. Everyone else is planet-side."

"This can't wait. You need to see and hear what happened with the demon prince. Meet me in the Echo chamber." Elija strode out of his room, resisting a temptation to ask the ship to show him Cindy-lu again. Surely she was fine.

Munna waited for him in the Echo chamber, manipulating a hologram of the collapsed seed vault and its surroundings. No imps remained outside. He glanced at Elija as he entered.

"The area's been cleared."

"Only of the living." Elija pointed to the bodies of the imps Munna had slain. "We should do something about those before the humans stumble across them." Even as he spoke, a light enveloped the carcasses and turned them to dust, the cantorii acting without a direct command. How many times had that happened before and he'd simply not noticed?

Munna gestured to the collapsed entrance. "What happened after I left? Visuals were unavailable when I beamed aboard."

"Astaroth set a trap."

"Obviously," Munna exclaimed with a roll of his eyes.

"It appears Astaroth not only knew of our

interest in the seed vault but that we'd have a baetylus for our quest. He somehow blocked our access to the ship after you were beamed and told us his plans. Let me see if my HALO managed to record anything." He ignited it and sighed as the events he'd lived through replayed from his perspective. Munna watched without blinking, a condensed version of it relayed to him via his HALO.

At the end, Munna whistled. "What a busy demon prince. Good thinking collapsing the building after fleeing into it."

"That wasn't me but Cindy-lu. She thought to use the mirror, and she's the one who managed to stab Astaroth when he attacked us in the vault."

"Wait, Astaroth was in the vault with you?"

It led to Elija explaining their time inside the vault, which his HALO hadn't caught since he'd not activated it.

At the end, Munna once more uttered a sound. "Sounds like quick thinking on Lulu's part."

"She's braver than many," he agreed.

"You appear unharmed. What of Lulu?"

"Fine. She's fretting over the seeds."

"At least the mission wasn't a complete failure.

"No, but I'm concerned about the fact that Astaroth lay in wait."

"It's not too surprising if you think about it. He's aware the Atlantis will need to supply if it's going to relocate humans, and the vault was the most logical place to get the required seeds."

"But how did he know we'd have a baetylus?" Because of those who knew, he'd never have expected any of them to tell.

"Most likely he sensed it and even if he didn't, he probably predicted we'd need one to transport." Munna shrugged. "I'd be more concerned about the fact he and his legion disappeared again while he had the signal blocked. By the time it resumed, there was nothing to see. Where are they hiding?"

"They must have a base of operation somewhere."

"How are they managing to move so stealthily? A horde that size should have shown up on our monitors." Munna flipped the holograms that floated, random images of the planet. "But there's nothing."

"Most likely he's using his blocking power to mask their movements."

"Which is going to impede our ability to decipher their location."

"That's not the only issue. This latest attack has proven he has more than just imps and demons at his disposal. On the surface, we encountered beasts that weren't naturally occurring."

"Which lends more credence to the idea he's got a secret lair where he's been building his army. The question is, how do we find it?"

"Find what?" Cindy-lu appeared suddenly in the Echo chamber.

Elija fought back a smile and an urge to go to her. He replied instead, "We don't know how to locate Astaroth and his legion."

Her nose crinkled. "He is a tricky jerk. But I'll leave hunting his ass to you. With Astaroth messing with our seed extraction, I've got my work cut out trying to decipher what we got and what we didn't. Plus, I need to figure out how we're going to get sperm and egg samples from the animals. So much to do..." she muttered, leaving as quickly as she came.

Not sparing much of a glance at him.

Not remembering what happened in that tent before the imps.

"Elija?" Munna snapped his fingers and drew his attention back.

"What?"

"We've got a new problem. The ship has been monitoring the planetary signals."

"And?"

"See for yourself."

The air changed to show Astaroth speaking, wearing a different suit from earlier and black gloves, one of them thicker than the other—on the same hand Cindy-lu had stabbed.

The Hell prince stood in a plain room, the walls blank but for a nail sticking out as if something used to hang there. He faced a camera and spoke with a slight tilt of his lips. It took a moment for his words to filter. "...incredible news to share with you. People of Earth, my name is Astaroth, and I am here today to announce that Hell is coming for your planet. Soon. So very, very soon. Why, if you turn your telescopes to the sky, you'll see it exiting your Milky Way and headed for your world. Now, your local governments and scientists have tried to convince you it's just an asteroid, and they'll probably also tell you that they can blow it up before it even comes close. But that is a lie. Hell is real, and its legions will bat your puny missiles out of the way. You cannot stop Hell. We will devour everything of worth on Earth. However, not all of you have to die. When Hell makes its grand arrival, a choice few will be selected to survive. Will you be one of them? And before you think we're looking for murderers and thieves only, let me assure you that there is room for all types. Do you have great ideas for innovation? Are you a scientist hamstrung by the rules on experimentation? Can you suck a golf ball through a garden hose? Because Hell is always in need of those with sexual expertise too. What we're not looking for are sanctimonious types. If you bring nothing to the table, then you will die. Horribly. Painfully. Don't believe me? Just ask the angels who've been hiding amongst you."

Video suddenly played, not just Aziel's first

excursion to Earth where he fought in full sight of humans filming, but also of the angels rescuing the scientists from Astaroth's castle where he'd been working to signal Hell. Then even more clips, so many videos of the angels thinking they weren't being seen, including one that showed them entering the base where they'd been working on evacuation ships.

Elija's mouth rounded in horror, and he murmured, "He knows about the hidden installation." They'd have to inform Metatron and evacuate. Before Elija could ignite his HALO and send a message to his principality, he realized Astaroth wasn't done.

"Now, you might be thinking, maybe the good guys will save the day. After all, angels are the righteous arms and weapons of God. Here's how many angels are on Earth." Each of their faces flipped quickly on the screen. A choir of nine.

"And here's how many I have to counter their annoying presence."

The screen flipped to show a horde of imps, flying and writhing on the screen, inside a massive space that crawled with their bodies. Then another oversized room appeared, this one hosting visible demons, foreheads projecting horns. Even they outnumbered the angels.

Astaroth reappeared. "As you can see, I have a great army, and that's just a fraction of what Hell will bring to Earth. Wait until the other princes arrive." His lips split into a wide smile. "Now that I've shown you the truth, time to run along, children of Earth. Scream. Cry. Kill. Beat your chests in futility. It's all you can do because God isn't coming to save you. All hail Lucifer."

The video of Astaroth ended.

Elija immediately tried to contact Metatron, only he didn't reply to his HALO. None of his brothers did. "We have to warn them."

Munna glanced at his injured wing. "I still can't fly."

"I can."

Munna's lips pinched. "Why bother being subtle and flying in from afar? They know about the base. There's no sense in hiding anymore." With that, Munna beamed away, and Elija was left alone.

Not entirely.

He spoke aloud. "Where is Cindy-lu?"

A brief glimpse of his room gave him all the direction he needed.

In moments, he'd entered and found Cindy-lu once more on his bed, this time, manipulating images in the air. Her nose wrinkled as she enlarged some for a better view and she muttered to herself.

She glanced at him and smiled. "Hey, hope you don't mind I borrowed your space." Her expression turned serious. "What's wrong?"

Rather than explain, he had the cantorii play Astaroth's message.

She watched it twice before saying, "He's trying to cause a panic by exposing everything."

"Will your people believe it?"

"Some will. Some won't. But as more evidence emerges of Hell's approach, I don't think it will be long before people realize he's telling part of the truth." Her lips turned down. "He just made our job even harder."

He'd also forced the angels' wings. Metatron had no sooner beamed aboard than he called a meeting that included some of the humans they'd been working with.

They all gathered in the common room to hear his words.

Metatron began with an ominous tone as he said, "By now you're all aware of the demon prince's actions. We now have a choice to make. We've already chosen to not destroy this planet as God commanded but rather help as many as we can escape. Given our mutiny against Elyon, we've kept our actions and presence quiet. However, with Astaroth's words today, we are now at a crossroads where we must decide if we will let him control the narrative with the flock or if we're going to reveal ourselves and counter the poison he's spewed."

"I know what my vote is," Munna muttered. "We can't let his lies stand."

"It seems like a simple choice," Eoch agreed.

"It is and isn't," Metatron continued. "By coming out into the open, we risk God finding out about our rebellion before we've had a chance to evacuate. We will make targets of ourselves not only with Heaven and Hell, but even humanity. Their history has shown they don't react well to outsiders."

"And every movie of alien encounters they have seems to end in their military trying to eradicate them all," Eoch complained.

"Those movies are fiction. This is real life, and people can be reasoned with. In this case, he might have done us a favor. It would be easier to accomplish our tasks if we had people cooperating with us," Cindy-lu stated.

Lilith, the first to meet an angel, nodded. "Agreed. Now that Astaroth has forced our hand, it's best if we swiftly counter with a message of our own. I'm thinking a few videos, where the angels reveal themselves and speak of our plans to help, would do much to counter his narrative. At the very least, it will move people to our side." She eyed Metatron. "As the choir leader, that would usually be a task that falls to you."

Metatron grimaced. "I'd rather be coordinating a defense."

To everyone's surprise, Leox cleared his throat. "I'll do it." Before anyone could protest, knowing how he felt about their disobedience to God, he hurried to add, "I swore to protect and guide the flocks. Not murder them so they couldn't get tempted by Hell."

"You might not be the boss, but as a spokes-angel, at least you're pretty," Lilith muttered. "Come. We want to get something to put out there recorded ASAP." She grabbed a bemused Leox by the arm, but Aziel, her mate, remained behind, arms crossed, looking grim.

Metatron began handing out orders. "Munna, since you're injured, you'll spend most of your time in the Echo chamber, alternating with Huud and monitoring for Astaroth as well as tracking Hell's approach. Also, see if you can contact the Atlantis and apprise them of the situation. Zakai will continue to assist Tamara as she devises a screening for passengers. Elija, you and Cindy-lu are to keep acquiring as many supplies as you can. The rest of you will be assisting the secret base in finishing those ships."

"It's not exactly secret anymore," muttered Jir.

"I'm aware, but we don't have time to relocate," Metatron countered. "I expect you'll also soon be coordinating with other agencies that might have space-capable vessels. You will do your best to assist."

"What of you?" Eoch asked.

Metatron's lips twisted as he said, "I will have the unenviable task of convincing the many governments that their only hope is to fight alongside us."

"And if they refuse?" a quiet question by Cindy-lu.

"Then we might not have a choice but to impose Angelic Law and take control."

CHAPTER 13

When the meeting broke up, I could see Elija remained perturbed. As we headed for his room, I kept quiet and wondered if he even wanted me around. After all, I'd made the assumption I'd be sharing his space. What if he wanted to be alone? I didn't want to come across as clingy or pushy.

When my step faltered, so did his, and he half turned, his gaze seeking out mine. "Is something wrong?"

"It occurs to me that I should have asked Zilla for another room."

"Why?"

I shrugged, suddenly feeling uncertain. "Because you might want your privacy."

He snorted. "Not from you."

I think that was a compliment? He ushered me

into his room, and while I stood there, he jumped to his perch and crouched.

"Going to sleep?" A disappointment, given not only was I too wound for rest but being in his room, with a bed, made me think of other things.

He shook his head. "Thinking. Do you really think people will pay heed to Astaroth's speech?"

"It's most likely trending hard right now on social media."

He grimaced. "My fault. If only I'd eliminated him when I had the chance."

I blew a rude noise. "What chance? When you were facing hundreds of his minions?"

"In the vault. I shouldn't have beamed. You'd injured him. It was the perfect opportunity."

"Maybe, but at the time, it seemed more important we get the talisman away from him."

He nodded. "True."

I then went on to say, "Look at the brighter side. By Metatron finally agreeing to go public, we might not have to sneak around to get the samples we need. People won't mock me when I say we need their seeds and eggs and sperm to save the world."

The statement curved his lips. "What kind of response do you usually get when you ask for sperm?"

"Why, Elija, are you teasing me?" I grinned. Who knew an angel could do a dirty flirt joke?

"I am doing and feeling many things because of you. And I am not sure I understand why."

"I do." I got close and reached to cup his cheek. "You like me."

A bashful look overcame him. and he glanced aside. "I shouldn't."

"It's all right if you do. Because I like you too. A lot." I reached on tiptoe, but he was just a little too high off the ground for me to reach. A good thing he had the strength to lift me so our lips could meet.

As we kissed, he murmured, "If being forsaken means a moment in your arms, then so be it."

Romantic and ominous all at once. My arms wrapped around him as he held me, but he wasn't content to just demurely kiss.

At his urging, my lips parted for the teasing foray of his tongue. A gentle suck and bite drew a groan and unleashed his passionate side.

He kissed me hard. Thoroughly. Sensuously.

I barely noticed when he leaped from his perch and carried me to his bed. Wrapped in the pleasure of his touch, I craved what would come next.

My back hit the mattress as he slowly lowered me. Our lips stayed connected. I never wanted to stop, even as I panted and couldn't catch my breath.

When he did break off the embrace, I uttered a sound of disappointment. Only to murmur in surprise as I opened my eyes to see him stripping. The shirt hit the floor first, revealing his wide shoulders, his bulky muscles leading to a sweet vee that disappeared into his pants. His flesh tempted me, and I beckoned, but he shook his head as he undid the ties to his pants and removed them as well.

He stood there proudly in front of me, his large cock jutting from his hairless groin. So much of him. I could have stared all day, only I wanted to touch.

My hands went to my own clothing, struggling to remove the annoying garments, only to huff with laughter as he took care of the problem by tearing them free. I would have protested, only I knew Zilla would take the remains and create new ones from them.

With us both naked, we came together, his body kneeling between my legs, his upper body leaning close enough I could place my palms flat on his skin. Warm. Smooth. His hard muscles twitched as I stroked over them.

I dragged him close to me for a kiss, the tips of my nipples poking his chest. Our lips clung, and I draped my arms around his shoulders as our embrace increased in intensity. His hand took a turn roaming my skin, while he used the other to proper himself up enough that he could explore.

I shivered and twitched at his touch, electrified by it. Wanting more.

Wanting him.

I only protested a moment when the kiss

stopped so that his lips could slide along my jaw then move to my neck.

He nuzzled me and sucked, even gently nipped, as if knowing my sensitive spot. I'd always been a sucker for necking.

But he didn't stay there for long. He moved down my body and paused over my breasts, staring at them, seeming uncertain.

"You can touch them," was my husky suggestion.

With a groan, he fell on me, his face rubbing the soft flesh of my breast, his lips dragging over already taut nipples. He teased and toyed with them, his hands clasping and squeezing, his expression ardent as he watched his own actions.

"I like having my nipples sucked." I offered in case he wasn't sure.

He cast me a quick glance before taking my advice. The flick of his tongue against a bud had me arching off his bed. Undaunted, he pinned my lower body with his before he once again lapped at my nipple. When he circled it with his tongue, I felt it between my legs.

I cried out when he sucked my breast into his mouth, my hips grinding and pushing against him. My nails dugs into his shoulder as he grazed the sensitive skin with his teeth.

The ache inside me grew and demanded satisfaction, but he didn't take the hint no matter how I groaned or wiggled. He remained fascinated by my tits.

So I gave him a nudge. "Kiss me."

He glanced at me, his eyes smoldering with passion, his lips tilting in a sexy grin. He then kept his gaze locked with mine as he dragged his mouth down the valley between my breasts, peppering me with kisses, that went lower and lower.

He paused at my pubes to murmur, "I would love to kiss you."

And he didn't mean my mouth.

I wasn't about to argue, but I did grab hold of his shoulders as he nestled between my legs and blew hotly on my cleft.

A good thing he held me pinned because that first lash of his tongue on my clit had me bucking hard.

He licked me, he sucked me, he teased me with his teeth and lips, and he had me coming before I could gasp *stop*.

I'd really wanted to have him inside me. But he didn't seem bothered I'd orgasmed without him. He kept licking me, dragging out my tiny climax and making my body tighten with need.

I sighed his name. "Oh, Elija."

It acted as a sign. He poised himself over my body. The head of his cock teased the entrance to my sex. Thick, so thick, but I welcomed the stretch as he eased himself into my tight sheath.

My pussy still trembled from my orgasm, and he gasped. A glance showed him strained as he tried to go slow. Tried to remain in control.

Cute but not what I wanted. My legs locked around his shanks and dragged him close, driving his cock deep, making us both gasp.

"Kiss me," I demanded as he held still inside as we both adjusted.

His mouth met mine in a torrid embrace as he began a thrusting rhythm. As we kissed, he slammed in and out of me, his cock butting against my inner sweet spot, making me tight with anticipation.

My legs fell to the side, widening his access, allowing him to drive deeper.

Faster.

Harder.

I could feel myself cresting again and couldn't hold in my cry of pleasure. I went rigid as my second, much more powerful, orgasm hit. It rolled through me like a tidal wave and dragged him in its wake. He thrust and held himself deep, the hot spurt of his pleasure only making my climax more intense.

I clung to him in the aftermath. Held him as if he'd fly away.

For now, he claimed to choose me, but would that change? I'd like to think I was the type of femme fatale who could lure a man away from God, but I knew my track record. I scared people off. I came on too strong. I had opinions. I was smart and not about to pretend otherwise.

Could Elija handle it?

He kissed me and said, "Yes."

I blinked. "Yes, what?"

I would have sworn I heard his reply in my head as he kissed me. *I chose you because you are all those things.*

CHAPTER 14

Elija left Cindy-lu sleeping in his bed. A petite female with the strength to bring him to his knees—and shift how he wanted to live.

He thought he'd known pleasure. Thought himself more virtuous than those who succumbed to carnal delight. Turned out he'd just not been with the right partner.

Cindy-lu engaged his senses in a way he'd not imagined. It was more than just the shape of her or the sounds she made as he touched her. It was how she viewed the world, fearlessly. How she dove into things with no care for herself or anything but the greater good. How she'd stayed behind to confront a monster to help him rather than escape.

A true warrior, one who wanted to be with him. And he would do anything to have a lifetime with her, which meant Hell couldn't be allowed to destroy what they had.

Despite the dire prediction of what Astaroth's video might accomplish, Elija had hoped the clip would disappear. A vain wish. Not only was it played over and over on what the humans called social media and on their news channels but people spoke of it in the streets, in their homes, along with the video Leox helped to make.

The devout Leox became the face of the angels, the messenger he called himself. He'd relayed a speech of hope.

"Fair citizens of Earth, my name is Leox. I am one of Elyon's elite warriors, and I am here to tell you God and his angels have not forsaken you."

Not the entire truth and Elija couldn't believe Leox managed to utter the lie. God had no part in this, and if he had his way, humanity would already be dead.

"Hell can only win if you let them. But you have the resources, the might, the will to combat the threat and prevail. However, it will require everyone, country and people alike, to come together to fight the forces of darkness."

For some reason, Leox's video garnered more skepticism than Astaroth's. People claimed his wings were fake. That the video clip he showed of Hell actually stripping a planet was something called CGI. The world declared a hoax until those manning telescopes reported back about the giant asteroid, the one that had abruptly veered its heading from the sun and now appeared on a collision course with Earth.

Governments did their best to calm the populace with platitudes. *"It will never reach." "It will miss." "We will destroy it."*

It did little to calm the panic. Riots broke out. Violence escalated, abetted by Astaroth, who let his imps loose. Winged demons began appearing in cities around the world. Swooping in to break windows and cause damage. Attacking people. Kidnapping children.

Soon there was no doubt in anyone's mind that Earth was in a crisis, which came to a head the day the Atlantis returned and hovered over North America, its massive shape bigger than anything Elija had ever seen. Bigger than all the other arks, surpassed in size only by Heaven itself.

Impressive. A beacon of hope for humankind.

And it almost got blown up by those Metatron had been negotiating with.

Jet fighters, mechanical planes armed with munitions, flew at the Atlantis, threatening to fire if the Atlantis didn't surrender.

The ark didn't negotiate. It beamed the planes aboard and returned only the pilots.

The show of its might didn't de-escalate the situation. People clamored for their governments to do something. *"Nuke it!" "Blast it with a virus!" "Give it what it wants before it kills us all!"*

Leox did his best to stem the wildest accusations—*"The aliens are here to conquer us."*

"Do not fear, but rejoice, for Elyon has gifted you with an ark that will provide a future for those chosen."

The wrong thing to say, as it led to arguing as to who should be saved. People screaming the process was unfair, even as it had barely started. The greedy at least made it easy to filter them out, as they tried bribes and threats to secure a spot.

To forestall violence against humanity's only hope, Metatron arranged a meeting with the president, a woman of severe countenance and a no-nonsense attitude that Cindy-lu confided had been the only thing that kept the country from splitting apart after years of contentious elections. Given the public's interest in the ark, the angels, and the future, the meeting was held at the White House. Outside its perimeter, thousands had gathered, held back by armored soldiers armed with guns.

Everyone wanted to see the angels in person. Many had come to plead for their lives.

Elijah found it hard to listen to, even as it strengthened his resolve. They were doing the right thing. God was wrong. Humanity deserved a chance.

The contingent of angels, comprising Metatron,

Elija, Zakai, and Aziel, arrived outside the White House grounds, beamed midair to the gasp of the people. Once the initial shock wore off, they began to chant and wave signs, although Elija had a hard time deciphering their complaints, as they appeared to cover a medley of causes, many of them unrelated to the threat at hand.

Cindy-lu travelled in his arms, his close partner since their excursion to the vault. He was never far from her side. When they weren't gathering specimens from around the world, they spent their time exploring each other, not just their bodies and desires, but their minds too. Their conversations could be spirited, given her vastly different perspective on things.

As they alighted, soldiers armed with projectile weapons aimed them in their direction.

Metatron held up his hands in a peace gesture. "Greetings. We mean no harm. We are here to converse with the president."

The crowd had hushed to hear him speak and now exploded into yells, many of them incoherent, and those that could be understood made no sense. *"No religion in our politics." "Down with the angeliarchy. Humans first." "Heaven, not Hell, is the enemy."*

Through it all, the angels stood proud, as did the humans who'd chosen to stand with them, more female than male, an oddity from the angel's perspective. Angel males had always been ever more populous, and as a result, the more gentle females had roles on Heaven that never had them dealing with the ugly that could exist elsewhere. The males were the protectors, the warriors against danger, the explorers and peacekeepers who kept the flocks that created the suul that Heaven needed in line.

But on Earth, men and women coexisted side by side, as partners, equals, and while it might have seemed strange at first, Elija no longer noticed. Not when Cindy-lu and the other women working with them added to their team dynamic in a way he'd have never expected.

Even Metatron appeared to have settled into a partnership role with a human woman of quick temper but fierce determination. Francesca led the templars—planet natives recruited by the choirs sent to shepherd. Although, in the case of the Earth templars, they'd strayed from their original mission and lost much lore once the choir went missing.

Together, the angels and their partners entered the White House, only to be halted before the doors by a soldier, who barked, "Drop your weapons."

Metatron crossed his arms and stated quite clearly. "No."

The soldier, a younger fellow with hair cropped close to his scalp, stiffened. "You can't go inside armed, sir."

"And I am telling you, *boy,* that I will not be

unarmed knowing the threat lurking on your planet."

Elija commended his principality on saying what he, and most likely the others, thought. Disarming them could be a trap.

At the same time, the soldier blocking their entrance wouldn't budge, and others had arrived, forming a loose line at their back. An attempt to fly would see them shot. Pushing past likely would result in the same.

It seemed they were at an impasse, which was when Francesca clapped her hands. "Bravo! You have both single-handedly handed this planet to Hell because you are too stupid to realize the angels with swords aren't the real threat." She shifted closer to the soldier denying them entrance. "Do you really think you could stop them if they chose to enter? They have a spaceship that can beam them anywhere. Weapons that can slice through thick metal. And they are the ones who will decide who gets to escape this planet on their ships from the coming destruction. But, sure, whip your dick around trying to prove it's not as small as your mind. After all, it's not as if you will be chosen. You've just proven you're unfit."

The soldier's face turned blotchy, and his finger slipped to the trigger of his weapon. Insulting him might not have had the effect Francesca hoped for.

"We'll see how cocky you are after spending time in lockup," the young male snarled.

"You're going to arrest us?" Lilith stepped forward. "For what? Calling out your bullshit. You're a little boy who has no idea of the gravity at hand, obviously, or you wouldn't be wasting our time. Tell you what. Since the president is more concerned about a semblance of safety than actually doing anything useful, how about we just leave? And when I say leave, I mean with the ark hovering overhead, you know the one that's supposed to save the children blah blah blah. There are plenty of people on this planet that would be happy to host us."

"Rules are rules," the dumb soldier insisted.

"Very well then, goodbye." Lilith waved a hand, and Aziel shrugged as he took her into his arms. HALOs ignited as they prepared to have the ship beam them. Metatron didn't protest. He slid an arm around Francesca's waist, and so Elija did the same with Cindy-lu.

The young soldier struggled to find words and then chose the wrong ones. "I forbid you from going. Arrest them!"

"Belay that order!" a stern, yet distinctly female voice shouted.

A woman pushed past the soldiers, and he whirled to complain, "Who are you..." He paused and blanched. "Madam President."

"Don't you madam president me when you

almost single-handedly ruined this meeting, which I asked for. Someone make him go away before he really does something we can't walk back from." The president waved a hand, and two other soldiers took the arms of the bullish one who kept protesting as he was led away.

"Sorry for his overzealousness. It's a pleasure to finally meet in person." The president apologized, and Elija got to study her from the side. She stood tall, her gaze almost on par with Elija's but not Aziel's and Metatron's, who both towered. Her gray hair had been pulled back into a ball at her nape, and she wore a dark outfit consisting of a jacket over a white shirt, pants that matched her outerwear, and flat-soled shoes.

"I am Metatron." The principality held out his hand in human fashion, and she clasped it without hesitation.

"People around here call me Madam President, but given you're a diplomat of sorts, I say we skip that part and go with Jane."

Metatron's eyes crinkled. "Well, Jane, shall we discuss how we're going to try and save the world?"

"I think that's a mighty fine idea."

With the president leading the way, the angels entered the White House, one of the most prestigious structures in the world, but Elija found himself underwhelmed. After all, he'd seen Heaven and its splendor; a place of plaster and stone just couldn't compare.

They were escorted to a large room, one set up with chairs and stools, the latter obviously being meant for the angels. A nice and welcoming touch that Elija ignored. He stood by the door they'd come in. Aziel opposite him, in line with the second exit they could see. Metatron chose to sit on a stool in the middle, his back to the windows as if he didn't care. He didn't need to; Zilla would be watching.

Elija and the other angels had taken to using the name Cindy-lu insisted on, even as they'd yet to talk to the cantorii directly. It came about because of Metatron, who, upon hearing Zilla's story, said, *"We should respect Zilla's wishes until we find out how to remove Elyon's block."* A block that Elija had a sneaking suspicious tied into their HALO.

The meeting began with the president casually saying, "So your adversary, Astaroth, has already visited me with an offer."

The surprise statement led to glances amongst the delegation.

A blank-faced Metatron drawled, "And?"

"And he's promised me, and others of my choosing, sanctuary on Hell in exchange for our promise we won't deploy the military against them."

"I hope you told him to fuck off." Lilith didn't temper her words, and Francesca snorted. "Took the words right out of my mouth."

President Jane's shoulders lifted slightly. "I told him I would consider his offer."

"You do know he's only saying that so you won't fight," Lilith pointed out, even as Metatron remained silent.

Jane shrugged. "I'm aware he can't be trusted. Just like I'm unsure if I should believe anything you say. After all, we only have your word that you're the better option. For all we know, this Heaven of yours is just as bad."

Lilith turned on Aziel to hiss, "Show her what happens when Hell decides it wants a planet's resources."

Metatron held up a hand and finally spoke. "Jane already knows. The proof of their perfidy was put at her disposal. She's aware Hell isn't to be trusted, which makes me wonder why you'd entertain Astaroth." The last he directed at the president.

She inclined her head. "Because it's never wise to let the enemy know what you think and always smart to let them blabber in case they reveal something. In this case, Astaroth seems to think he can negotiate for Hell, which is interesting seeing as how he's had no contact with them for centuries. Seems to me like he's in no position to bargain."

"Meaning what? You'd bargain with a different, more well-connected, Hell prince?" Francesca accused.

Jane remained calm. "Before you get overly

angry, keep in mind it is my job to look at and listen to all sides. Decisions I make don't affect just me but millions in the USA, billions if I count the world. It means I must weigh all options carefully."

"You've already come to a decision." It was Cindy-lu who murmured aloud. "And before we've even had a chance to argue our case."

"Argue what? I agree we need to evacuate as many as we can with supplies in the hope that if the fight goes wrong not everyone is lost. The world has been talking about colonizing other worlds. We just lacked the ability to do so until now."

"So you'll help us?" Cindy-lu asked.

"As much as we can. Explaining that the plan is to evacuate people from every culture will hopefully ease some of the friction that's aroused in other countries due to religious differences."

Elija understood what Jane meant, only because Cindy-lu had explained it to him. *"Not everyone believes in your God. Religion is a very hot topic in some places, with very strict beliefs and rules. There are some that will refuse to even listen because of it."*

"That would be most useful," Metatron stated. "Thank you."

"But that's only part of the reason for this meeting. While evacuation is all well and good, we all know it's only going to benefit a few. Billions will be left behind. Billions who will die unless we fight."

"Fight?" Francesca repeated the word.

"Did you really think I'd give in to blackmail from someone like Astaroth?" Jane's expression turned hard. "I let him talk and sent him on his way. I then invited you here not to negotiate but to tell you how it's going to be. We are going to evacuate as many young people and adults with useful skills as we can. We will provide you with all the supplies you need. Food, clothing—"

Metatron interrupted. "Will be provided. What we require are seeds for the colony once it arrives. Genetic sampling of creatures as well to ensure an adequate food source."

Jane nodded. "That's actually good to know, as it means we'll have more resources to devote to keeping the citizens in line. The whole picking process isn't going to be easy. Parents will beg for their children to be saved. Young and old will argue why their lives are worth saving over others." She shook her head. "The ugly in people will come out. I wish people would look past their own needs for once and be respectful of a difficult process; however, we are, after all, human." She offered a wry smile.

Metatron returned it. "We will try to be quick and discreet with the process."

"I'm sure you will, but that's not the only reason we needed to talk. While the supplying of the ark is going on, we also need to be planning for the coming conflict. With nothing to lose, we might as well fight. We have been working on lines of defense and attack that will, of course, adapt to take into account your contribution. We'll need to know weaponry and intel you'll bring to the conflict so we can incorporate it into our plan."

It led to the angels eyeing each other before Metatron admitted, "We have only ourselves and our blades."

Jane blinked in surprise. "Surely your ship is armed to fight."

"The arks and cantorii are meant for exploration and colonization. They do not have a means of attacking or even defense." Metatron didn't lie.

"But someone said something about a beam of light?" The president appeared flustered by the reply.

"Heaven's flame cannot be used in war."

"Then I'm going to be blunt. What do you bring to this alliance?"

"Knowledge and a willingness to stand by your side."

Jane's lips pursed. "I'd hoped for more like a super weapon that could do damage to this Hell ship."

Her disappointment led Elija to say, "Your nuclear missiles are greater than anything I've ever heard of."

"Wait, are you saying you haven't discovered

nukes?" She stared open-mouthed at them then sighed. "It would seem I have much to learn."

"As do we. But together, I believe we might be able to achieve the impossible." Metatron stated, as if it were the truth.

And maybe it was. Elija could only hope they would prevail because anything else would mean an end to the happiness he'd found.

CHAPTER 15

Having the Atlantis hovering for everyone to see dispelled much of the rhetoric about the whole Hell and angel thing being a hoax. Kind of hard to deny when a massive spaceship hovered over a sizeable portion of the Nevada desert.

Its appearance meant I finally got the cooperation I needed to ensure a wide selection of seeds and genetic samples. Although I would note that not everyone donated. Some of the more religiously devout countries in the Middle East abstained; however, I didn't let their recalcitrance bring me down. Not with the clock ticking.

We were seven months before Hell arrived, and the ark needed to be long gone before then. Even now, I could see Elija and the others stressing about the fact they'd not encountered any of Hell's advance scouts.

ELIJA

"Is that unusual?" I'd asked, given I could see the stress in his face as he returned from yet another meeting.

"Very," Elija had replied.

"Maybe their ships are slower moving than you expected."

He'd shaken his head. "I've encountered them before. They are as fast, if not faster than the cantorii."

"Could be they're being cautious."

"Or they're here already and plotting."

An ominous possibility that I left to Elija and the others to figure out. My task wasn't the defense of the planet but the survival of humanity once they left it.

Given my part of the job appeared to be moving along smoothly, with donations being coordinated ahead of time—where those giving were told to place the bins in an open area for beaming—I found myself with extra time on my hands. I chose to use it to help Tamara, who was swamped with applications.

Poor Tamara. She'd done her best to streamline the process, putting the questionnaire to apply online, and providing it on paper to those who couldn't access the internet. Only those chosen from the thousands upon thousands got called to do in-person interviews. Interviews that she at least delegated to others. However, the entire thing took a toll on Tamara.

She'd sobbed more than a few times, *"I hate having to choose. Why can't we take them all?"*

Her soft heart wanted to help everyone, but the reality was the ark could only take a limited number. To those not selected but who made it to the interview, we offered the option to have their eggs or sperm harvested.

Needless to say, none of it went over well. People took to social media to rant that God had forsaken them. That the angels were evil for not saving everyone. The vitriol proved especially nasty to those of us actively helping them. They called us whores because we dared to love a man with wings. They called us traitors to humankind. Said that we were spreading our legs to secure a spot. Nothing could be further from the truth.

I had resigned myself to the fact I wouldn't be going with the ark when it left. Even a spot on Zilla wasn't assured. While Zilla and I appeared to have a bond, I remained well aware she wasn't mine to order or control.

For the moment, I basked in the affection I shared with Elijah but remained cognizant of the fact he might leave—without me. From the conversations we'd had, I knew angels didn't technically marry. They paired up romantically, sometimes choosing to share space, other times keeping it more separate and casual. I'd been too chicken to ask him if angels loved. And if yes, was that love fleeting?

After all, when you can travel the stars and see wonders in other galaxies, why would you want to stick around to watch a planet get pummeled into oblivion?

Such depressing ruminations weren't my usual thing, and I did my best to ignore the nagging voice in my head that insisted he'd abandon me. I couldn't let my love life affect my focus on the situation at hand.

As Hell neared, tension levels rose. As expected, panic erupted and brought with it violence and anarchy. Looting became widespread, as did murders—with some people claiming they did it to curry favor with Hell. Entire sections of cities became no-go zones, as some ethnic groups chose to close ranks and declare themselves autonomous. Rumor further stated some of them thought they could negotiate with Hell for spots.

To them, I said good luck. At least we didn't have to worry about them adding to our pile of applicants.

During all this, the Atlantis and its mysterious commander, Noah, hadn't spoken much. Tamara, the only person Noah would talk with, claimed his ship was busy preparing and had been taking most of what I'd collected, but not all. Apparently, the Atlantis still had samples left over from the last time there was a flood. As a joke, I'd said to Tamara, *"Did he find the missing unicorn DNA?"* to which Zilla had been the one to reply, *"Unfortunately the creature you referenced ran off before he could collect any."*

Well, shit. Not the reply I expected.

The oddest twist in this whole debacle came from certain media outlets. I shouldn't have been surprised given their propensity for click-bait pieces. Anything to get people watching and bringing in those advertising dollars. What I never expected was that some of them would fall on the wrong side. They dubbed the approaching menace Planet Hell and kept inviting Astaroth to their segments so he could talk about how great it was. How there were none of the strict rules that bound Earth's population. No mega God lording over them all but a bunch of princes who welcomed new citizens and wouldn't judge them harshly like Elyon and the angels would. Astaroth painted a picture of a decadent place where pleasure and fantasies could come true.

I'd asked Elija about it. "Is anything coming out of his mouth true?"

To which my angel lover shook his head and murmured, "The pleasure he speaks of isn't for the slaves they'll take. The Hell princes and their courts live lavishly. But everyone else..." He shrugged.

Everyone else would struggle to survive. Many would die. There was a reason Hell kept looking for newer planets to steal from. They destroyed more than they created.

ELIJA

A break in my tasks arrived in the form of Paola from my ancient Novae team, currently overseeing those working on the two starships in our once-hidden bunker. She wanted me to come critique the hydroponics system they'd installed.

At first, Elija refused. "I'd rather you didn't go. It's too dangerous. Astaroth knows about the base."

Overprotective instinct? Super cute, especially since I'd never had a guy want to coddle me before. However, being a modern woman meant he didn't get to decide for me.

"Astaroth has had weeks to do something about it. There hasn't been a single sighting of an imp in the area."

"He might be biding his time."

"And so what if he is? I can't hide away forever. Not to mention, we need every ship we can get in the sky. Which, again, won't be worth diddly-squat if they aren't self-sustaining."

"Why can't the team there run the tests?"

"They have, but I'm the one who designed the system. They want me to give it a proper look-over to make sure they haven't messed up any of my specs." And to be honest, I was ready to see something other than Zilla's walls. The cantorii was a nice ship, don't get me wrong, but I missed being able to go outside, breathe in fresh air, feel the sun on my face.

"You're not going without me."

"Are you sure they can spare you? I thought Aziel and you were giving a demonstration to the troops on how to fight the imps and demons." Because two-legged humans had a disadvantage when it came to those with wings.

He grimaced. "Maybe Munna can take my place."

"Munna's wing is almost healed. He'd be dumb to stress it now. How about, instead, Munna accompanies me and you go do your thing with Aziel."

He frowned. "I don't like that idea. I should be the one protecting you."

The sweetest thing ever said, and truth be told, I'd prefer him by my side, but at the same time, I didn't want to be that woman who clung and didn't allow her partner to accomplish the things he needed to do.

"I'll be fine. I'll only be gone a few hours."

He winced. "That long?"

I couldn't help but smile. We'd been inseparable these last few weeks, and I'd never been happier. Elija gave me something I'd been longing for in my life—someone who accepted me as I was. He didn't expect me to put on some act, dress a certain way, or dumb down my intelligence. He liked me, dare I say even loved me, and boy could he make my body sing.

"I'll miss you too."

He dragged me close for a kiss, murmuring

between nibbles, "Be careful. Any sign of trouble, you tell Zilla to get you out of there."

"Yes, dear." I laughed. "You be careful too."

We separated after that, him off to do a training exercise and me to the surface with Munna.

"Thank you for getting me off the cantorii. I could use the break," he admitted as we turned our faces to capture the sun's rays.

"You should have heard Elija try and talk me out of it."

"He threatened to clip my wings if any harm came to your person."

"He did not!"

"He is very fond of you."

"The feeling is mutual."

Since we no longer needed to hide, Zilla transported us only yards from the mountain hiding the base. It was exactly as I recalled, a non-descript rocky mound with no sign of life from the outside.

As we strode for the hidden door, I grimaced. Despite what I'd told Elija, I wasn't keen on going back inside. The entire time I'd spent here previously I'd been aware of the cloying and pressing weight of the concrete and mountain surrounding me. The claim that it was mostly bomb-proof didn't alleviate that anxiety much, especially since I knew the hangar doors could be penetrated. They were the weakest point of the structure because, after all, we needed a way for the spaceships to blast their way out.

The main entrance, hidden behind some rocks, had a soldier guarding it, a templar knight judging by the badge on his chest. He gave us a nod and opened the door to give us access. Before it closed, I heard him speaking into his walkie-talkie. "Angel and scientist incoming."

The thud as the heavy door shut made me startle, and my palms began to sweat. Silly reaction. I could easily turn around and walk back out.

Munna noticed my disquiet. "You all right?"

"Yeah. Blame Elija for making me jumpy. He made it seem like I was walking into dire danger."

"He's worried because he cares."

"He's also paranoid."

"Not exactly. He's right to suspect the Hell prince is plotting."

I snorted. "Plotting, yes, but I'm pretty sure I'm far from Astaroth's mind." A month since our encounter at the vault and I'd not had a single sighting of him or his minions the few times I'd been back to Earth.

Back to Earth. Never thought I'd ever think it, let alone have it happen. Yet it shouldn't have been so strange. I'd spent the last decade working on a project meant to do exactly that. And now, I was on the cusp of seeing it come to fruition.

"Let's go see my ships." I led the way to the

hangar, one enormous space with two vessels lying horizontal for the moment. Once we deemed them ready, they'd be lifted into a vertical position and tied to the rockets that would blast them past our atmosphere.

We'd come a long way in the months since we'd first started. The half-built spaceships in the abandoned military installation needed a total overhaul of their electronics and a lot of stress testing to ensure welds, and other aspects, were solid enough to handle the pressure of space. We'd also had to retrofit parts of it to implement not only a better air circulation system but the hydroponics system that would allow those on board to grow fresh vegetables and fruit, as well as compost all waste to be reused. Once launched, there would be nowhere for them to grab supplies. The ship had to be self-sustaining.

I entered the first of the ships, named Eden One, a craft that should be able to carry fifty people. A drop in the grand scheme of things but still, between it and Eden Two, it meant a hundred more people could escape.

If everything worked.

Unlike the ark, these ships would be taking adults with the skills needed to keep everything working. Welders, electricians, mechanics. Anyone with the ability to fix and innovate to keep things running would have a chance at a spot starting with the people in this base. They'd worked hard and deserved it.

But I wouldn't be one of them. Not because it wasn't offered. I'd declined because I knew Elija wouldn't fit in the tight halls and small cabins and I wouldn't abandon him. Was I being foolish by refusing to go?

No, I was in love.

I spent the next two hours inspecting the system. I'd already studied all the data from the test runs. From all appearances, everything worked as it should. On the ground. I could only hope it continued once it got to space.

As I exited the vessel, I noticed Munna staring at the roof overhead and frowning.

"What's wrong?"

"Do you hear that?"

I listened and shook my head. "I don't hear anything. Might be maintenance, though. I know they were talking about testing the doors soon seeing as how we're almost done."

"Those tests were run a week ago," Munna stated, lips still pursed.

It was then I saw it, the sifting of dust coming from above. It led my gaze upward just as a whine started to vibrate the hangar doors. A whine of something trying to pierce metal.

"Someone's trying to get into the base!" I yelled, running for Munna, only to fall as an explosion rocked the mountain. I hit the floor and covered my head as debris fell.

"Lulu!" Munna shouted my name in the ensuing chaos of sirens and dust. I blinked gritty lashes trying to see, and then wasn't sure I wanted to, as I heard screams mixed with the hissing excitement of imps.

Imps in the hangar with me.

Yikes.

I crawled, looking for cover, and tried calling Zilla. *"Help. We need out of here."*

No reply, which chilled me because that could mean only one thing.

Astaroth.

As if thinking about him conjured the man, I heard him drawl, "Going somewhere?"

I flipped around to see nothing. Yet I knew Astaroth stood nearby, hiding within his damnable cloak.

My hand fumbled for the dagger Elija insisted I wear at all times. Before I could firmly grip it, a booted foot kicked it from my grip.

"No sharp things for you, Cindy-lu," he mocked. "Not after what you did to me last time." A hand emerged, the fingers crooked like claws, the angry red scarring a reminder of what I'd done.

Of why he was pissed.

"What do you want?" I blustered with more bravery than I felt.

"Revenge for one. You don't need your hands for what I have planned." With that threat, he pushed back the hood and smiled at me. "Fear not, I'll leave your mouth intact, although I might remove your tongue."

Okay, forget faking bravery. I scrabbled away from him as he did the slow stalk. I felt very much like one of those terrified heroines in a movie knowing I had nowhere to hide. Nothing to save me.

I also kept foolishly waiting for Elijah to appear to the rescue. After all, I had a guardian angel, with a great big sword. Any second now, he'd come swooping in and handle Astaroth once and for all.

Elijah didn't appear, and when Astaroth waved a hand and ordered, "Bring her to the lair," I was no match for the burly demons with their human sneers, curling horns, and meaty fists. One clock to the head and I was seeing stars—the concussion kind. It sapped my ability to fight.

Clawed paws gripped my arms, an imp on each side. Together they lifted me into the air, dangling me between them, putting just enough tension I feared they'd tear me apart.

But nothing compared to my terror as they flew away.

CHAPTER 16

Having combat experience didn't mean much with Elija's concentration being off. Aziel knocked his blade easily aside as they presented their demonstration to the human soldiers.

They'd been at it for hours now, one of them being the imp/demon swooping in on a soldier, the other playing a human on the ground, to an avid crowd taking mental notes. Not that it started out that way. In the first few minutes, there'd been much sniggering by the soldiers. One in particular had been loud.

"Not sure why you're showing us how to fight hand-to-claw when we can just shoot the fuckers out of the air." The short-haired recruit indicated by waggling his rifle.

An observation to which Aziel offered a cold smile. "Oh really? Let's see how your combustion weapon does against me." Aziel held out his arms, and his HALO ignited. *"Go ahead and fire."*

"I ain't going to shoot you. My fucking lieutenant would have my ass," the brash fellow declared with a shake of his head.

"You won't get into trouble, as I am ordering you to fire upon me. Now or you will see what happens to those who don't obey orders."

"But— I can't—" the man blustered, no longer so brash.

"Are not words that should come out of a soldier's mouth. Will you also refuse to fight in a battle?" Aziel drew his sword, and as if it knew it were on display, it appeared darker than usual, while glowing at the same time, the divinii-forged blade eager to engage.

The soldier swallowed hard. "If I shoot and accidentally kill you, I'm gonna get thrown in the brig."

"Shoot!" Aziel commanded, his sword slowly lifting as he darted on foot for the soldier.

In a sudden panic, the one about to learn a lesson lifted his weapon and pulled the trigger. Bang. The bullet went straight. Would have gotten Aziel in the upper shoulder if it didn't bounce from his flesh.

Aziel kept coming.

The soldier began shooting in quick succession, his aim jerking around as he stumbled away from the charging angel.

Bang. Bang.

Not one bullet penetrated Aziel's personal shield.

Part of their HALO defense system, it could repel most blows. Few things could penetrate it. A human-made bullet not being one of those things.

The soldier gaped as Aziel didn't pause as he swung his blade, shearing the barrel of the gun. The muzzle hit the ground amidst the silence of the watching troops, and Aziel finally paused his movement, arms lifted, blade at the soldier's neck.

A clear victor.

The silence held a hint of awe that shattered with a drawled, "Holy fuck."

With their attention snared by admiration, Aziel stared down the soldier receiving the lesson. "It is time you listened and took what I'm saying seriously. You aren't going to be fighting just humans but Hell's legion. They will have many tricks."

"Wait, what do you mean we'll be fighting our own kind? Thought our beef was with the devil?" asked a female soldier that had caused Elija some pause when he first realized they were part of the troops sent to learn. Heaven didn't have any female soldiers. But humans were different in so many ways.

"Surely you've been paying attention." Elija inserted himself into the lecture. "Your planet has billions of people who already are at odds sometimes over the most minor things. Do you really think that all of the world's population will be aiding in our effort to repel Hell?"

"I can think of a few I know that would sell their mothers to be in the devil's army," quipped a slim fellow

with freckled skin and the orangey hair Elija had never seen outside of Earth.

"There are always those of your own kind that will oppose you. You might have to fight them." Elija paused then added. "You might also have to kill. Not just humans that might confront you but imps and demons, who might look human. The higher levels can change their appearance to match the populace."

"Fucking shapeshifting demons! And what the fuck do we have?" exclaimed a different woman.

"You can die or you can fight. There are no other choices," Aziel stated firmly.

"You just said some people are going to join with Hell."

"They will try," Elija agreed. "But Hell isn't a place you can just decide to belong to. Hell is particular who it takes. It depends on where it thinks you'll be most useful. Laborer? Because machines can't do everything. Cook and clean? A fighter for their many entertainment clubs? Or perhaps you're more of a whore? Always a large demand for those." He let his gaze roam. "Which of you is willing to give up the life you have now to become Hell's slave?"

Feet shuffled, fabric rustled, and heads turned side to side as the soldiers regarded each other in discomfort.

"Do you really think we can fight?" the first female soldier asked.

Aziel nodded. "You wouldn't be the first planet to manage to repel Hell. There are entire galaxies we are forbidden to visit because they've erected strong defenses that don't allow for outsiders."

"Meaning we can fucking do this," The red-haired soldier stated, punching the air.

"But how?" asked a serious male in the front. "We couldn't even shoot you."

"Because of my shield. Which only the demons will have. The imps are a more basic version and can be taken out with guns and in hand-to-hand combat," Aziel explained.

Elija jumped in. "Gases can affect them, the problem being ensuring your own troops have protection against anything used."

"But not the demons?" The somber female soldier spoke again. "If they shield, how are we supposed to stop them?"

"By wearing them down and not dying while you do it." Aziel told them the blunt truth. "The shields can't be held for too long, given how much power they take. Demons especially don't have large reserves compared to angels. Once their power source is depleted, they can be harmed by normal means."

"How do they regenerate?" The woman asked another good question.

"By killing and taking the suul from flesh before it escapes."

"That's like horror-movie-level shit." The new voice held a hint of awe.

"How do we know their shield is down? Do they have a glowing thing like your HALO?" The woman pointed.

Elija shook his head. "There is no way of seeing it, but you can somewhat be prepared when they either try to escape or turn rabid in their attack."

"To weaken them, strike, and strike often, so they don't release the shield and run out of power quickly," Aziel advised. *"If you watch carefully, I will show you where to strike to incapacitate them quickly. Also, stay out of reach of their claws. Wounds gouged by them tend to fester."*

After that, the troops watched much more ardently. Even once they got to practicing, their focus remained honed.

Better than Elija's. The longer he spent away from Cindy-lu, the more his unease increased. He couldn't explain it. They'd been separated before but on the ship, each working on different tasks at once. But now she was off somewhere else on the planet. Without him.

She has Munna.

Munna wasn't Elija.

Aziel sparred with Elija to give the soldiers an example of bladework that did take into account flight. Aziel dove from the sky, sword point extended. Elija performed a sloppy slap and then misstepped, his stumble almost costing his arm. Aziel stopped short of shearing it.

Elija regained his footing easily, but Aziel growled, "What's wrong with you?"

He opened his mouth to say "I don't know." but his tongue knew otherwise. "Something's amiss. I think Cindy-lu's in trouble." The moment he said it, it hit with a sickening certainty.

Rather than mock his concern, Aziel glanced at the woman who'd asked all the questions. "Excuse while I attend to a matter." Aziel led Elija away from the practicing troops and, as an added caution, spoken in Heaven's language. "Did Cindy-lu contact you?"

He shook his head. "It's more of a feeling."

"You are quite close. Like me and Lilith." Stated, not asked.

He shrugged. "I guess. We share a room. Have sex."

"I hear a but."

It took Elija a moment to articulate himself. "I care for her a great deal, but I am well aware it can't last forever. What future do we have? If I put her on the ark to save her, I might never see her again. If I keep her here for the fight, she might die."

Aziel arched a brow. "Already assuming we'll lose?"

"More like realistic about our chances." He paused then asked, "Do you not worry about Lilith?"

"Every moment of every day. At times, I am

certain the right thing to do is to stow her aboard Zilla and demand we fly far from here."

A feeling Elija well understood. "Why haven't you?"

"Because she would hate me for being cowardly and leaving her world to suffer."

Elija sighed. "Sounds like Cindy-lu."

"It isn't easy being in love with strong, admirable women."

"Love?" He blinked as he said the word. "Is this what I'm feeling?" For an angel who'd counseled others, including Zakai, on embracing love, he realized now that he'd never fully known it himself. The only love he'd been sure of was that for God, but Elyon didn't make him feel anxious when apart or fulfilled when together. Not to mention, he'd forsaken his God because of Cindy-lu.

"We've been conditioned our entire lives to think we have only one purpose, serving Heaven. Keeping Heaven safe. Making Heaven prosperous. Strengthening God. Spreading order. And there was a time that was enough. Then I met Lilith—"

Elija interrupted to blurt out, "And you realize there can be another way. One that makes you excited to wake, that consumes your thoughts, but in a good way."

"Exactly." Aziel nodded in agreement. "If it helps, at first, I didn't understand how I felt. What I felt. But once you accept it and, even better, commit to it, it becomes the most fulfilling thing you can imagine." Aziel appeared almost reverent as he said it.

"If we do prevail against Hell, what will happen to us? Will we return to Heaven? Stay here on Earth? Go somewhere new?" Questions he'd asked himself, wondering which path he wanted.

"I think it's pretty clear that we can't go back to Heaven."

"What if God declared he'd forgive our trespasses?"

A snort escaped Aziel. "We both know that won't happen. And even if Elyon did decide to not smite, I wouldn't leave Lilith to return, nor would I subject her to Heaven. We both know how she'd be treated."

As a womb for harvesting with no access to anything but the breeding and creche locations. She couldn't even go for a walk outside those facility walls. Non-angels had no rights on Heaven.

"If we can't go to Heaven, then where?"

"If it's not destroyed, we could stay on Eden. Or we could remain with Zilla and follow the Atlantis to a brand-new world. Perhaps explore other places if Zilla agrees."

"But only if we prevail against Hell," Elija's ominous addition.

Because only in victory could they hope to live in happiness and love.

His HALO pinged, demanding he activate it.

He glanced at Aziel, who had his already blazing. He ignited the HALO to hear Munna exclaiming, "...attacked. The human transport ships have been destroyed. The entire base is being evacuated."

Elija's blood ran cold. "What of Cindy-lu? Is she back on Zilla? Is she safe?"

Munna paused. "I'm sorry, Elija. I couldn't find her in the aftermath."

CHAPTER 17

Hearing that Cindy-lu couldn't be located stopped Elija's heart. "Is she dead?" The query curdled in his mouth.

"I don't think so." Munna hesitated before adding, "Her body isn't here, and one of the survivors claims to have seen her in the grip of imps, being flown away."

"They took her?" That might be a fate worse than death. "I have to find her." Elija shut out Munna to contact the cantorii. "Beam me to the base at once."

Bright light enveloped him, and he had a moment of discombobulation before he reassembled in the requested spot. He arrived midair, plummeting for a few brief seconds before his wings unfurled with a snap. He didn't fly alone. Aziel had also beamed.

The archangel spoke via his HALO. "I see people exiting. Going to check it out." Aziel dove for the ground.

Elija didn't follow, as he scouted the situation. His vantage point had him high enough to see the damage wrought to the top of the mountain. Plumes of smoke rose from the mountain, emerging from the hole blasted through its peak. He knew from his time at the base that there used to be access doors in that location, direct access to the hangar where Cindy-lu was supposed to be working. A siren wailed, making it impossible to make out audible details.

With his HALO blazing, Elija called forth his shield, not worried about depleting it. Only demons needed to kill to regenerate. HALOs usually recuperated slowly on their own, very slowly, unless God or a Jesus Christ chose to give it a boost. But here on Earth, that hadn't been the case. His HALO had never been more powerful, and it didn't seem to be close to running out. Zakai opined that the plentiful suul on the surface accounted for that difference, the HALO easily recharging in the suul-dense atmosphere.

With his shield protecting should there still be enemy, and to avoid breathing in what could be caustic air, Elija arrowed for the smoking opening, diving down past the twisted metal that remained of the blasted doors and dropping into the massive chamber, only to pull up short as he eyed the destruction.

The two ships pulverized in their berths, holes gaping from them, as if exploded from within. Burning and reeking of melting components. Utterly ruined and unusable, also clearly an act of sabotage.

Moving more cautiously, he hovered over the wreckage of the ships, his wings fanning the smoke that humans appeared to be making worse as they aimed red canisters that shot white foam at smoldering spots. He couldn't see why they bothered. There would be no salvaging these remains. No escape for the humans who'd worked diligently on them. Astaroth's minions had destroyed that hope.

Despite Munna's claim of an eyewitness seeing Cindy-lu being kidnapped, Elija dipped and swerved, his keen eyes seeking, his heart stilling whenever he saw a body lying prone. He searched in vain. That realization had him landing near Munna, who handled the downed imps, slicing off their heads, ensuring they didn't feign death and later pose a threat. Those who called it harsh had never seen a village slaughtered because of a single imp left alive after an attack.

Elija landed and barked, "What happened?"

His brother turned a bleak expression on him. "Imp attack."

"Obviously. How did they get inside?" He pointed. "There's supposed to be surveillance at the mountain peak at all times." That had always been the case when he'd been stationed here briefly.

Munna shrugged. "I don't know what happened to those watching. All I do know is we had no warning. One minute, Lulu was exiting a ship, and the next, an explosion hit. Smoke and dust made it impossible to see much. The imps used that to hide their attack."

"Brazen." He grunted. "And you're sure they took Lulu?"

"A coworker of hers, you probably remember her, Paola, claims she saw her being taken by a pair." Paola wasn't the type to be mistaken or exaggerate what she'd seen.

"If she was taken by imps and not immediately killed, then that means Astaroth wanted her." He recalled all too well what the demon prince had taunted the last time they'd met. How Astaroth planned to defile her.

"Alive is better than dead," Munna stated. "That means we can mount a rescue to save her."

Save, yes. That went without saying. However, what if she suffered already? What if he arrived too late?

He clenched his fists against the chilling rage that swept him. So much for being an unemotional soldier. It wasn't so easy when someone he loved faced dire danger. "We have to find her quickly."

"Agreed. But where do we start our search? They

arrived in stealth and left the same way." Munna's shoulders slumped in dejection.

Just like in Norway. As if they could teleport, and if that were the case, they could be anywhere. A daunting realization. However, Elija wouldn't allow himself to give in to defeat. There had to be a way to find her. This was his fault. He'd left her alone, against his better judgment, and look what happened. Cindy-lu went missing, taken prisoner by a sadistic Hell prince. In danger. Possibly dead. Likely hurting.

It led to him bellowing, "Astaroth, I am coming for you!" The prince didn't offer a reply, but a human did.

A smudge-faced Tamara appeared, along with Zakai, wielding one of the red canisters.

"What are you doing here?" he asked. Last he'd heard, the pair had been aboard the Atlantis coordinating the incoming refugees.

"We came to help as soon as I heard of the attack." Zakai glanced around. "This will be a blow to the cause."

As if Elija cared about that. "They took Cindy-lu."

Tamara cleared her throat. "I know. Zilla told me. She had a feeling something was wrong the minute she lost contact with Cindy-lu. She believes it's either because Cindy-lu is locked somewhere with heavy shielding or Astaroth is nearby casting a null field."

Wait, the cantorii knew? "Why didn't the ship notify me?" he huffed.

Tamara rolled her shoulders. "She tried, but as you know, Zilla is blocked from dealing with angels directly. She can only respond to orders."

His lips pinched. "She had no issue contacting you."

"Because I don't have a HALO blocking communication." Tamara canted her head as if listening to someone. "Speaking of HALO, Zilla says you might want to shut off yours because the prince is listening."

Elija gaped but immediately extinguished it before asking, "Why does she think the Hell prince can spy on us via our HALOs?"

"Because they're compromised. The Hell prince has found a way to listen in."

"How do we stop it?" Elija asked.

Zakai, not surprisingly, had the answer. "Remove it."

Remove his HALO? His fingertips went to his head as if he could feel it. He couldn't. None of them could. When they were lifted from the creche and given their role as warriors, God blessed them with the circlet of light. It was their reward. A tool. And also it now appeared a way of watching them, not just by Elyon and Heaven but the enemy as well.

He eyed his brother. An angel with wings but no HALO. "You got rid of yours after your mission to find the Atlantis. Why?"

Zakai's lips twisted. "Because I've long suspected it wasn't the blessing we were taught."

"Why didn't you tell us so?"

He rolled his shoulders. "My belief in something doesn't make it true. I couldn't be sure if it was my paranoia due to my past experience."

Elija could understand that reasoning. But at the same time, the theory would explain so much. Why Astaroth always seemed to know more than he should. How he kept appearing where he shouldn't.

If he went after the demon prince, would his HALO give warning? Would he then walk into a trap?

"Do you also speak directly with the cantorii?"

Zakai hesitated a fraction of a second before nodding. "Yes, and it's been interesting."

"And you never told me." Stated, not asked.

"We've all been so busy. Which is a bad excuse. I know."

He wanted to be mad at his brother but couldn't. "I think there is much for us all to still learn that we've long taken for truth." Like the fact that not everything was as simple as God and Heaven wanted to make things out to be. Perhaps it was time to start forging his own path. He knew where to start. He tapped his temple. "How did you remove your HALO?"

Zakai's lips turned down. "Not easily. It's a painful procedure. You'll lose much that you're used to and know that, once it's gone, without God involved, it can't simply be put back."

"I won't have my shield anymore." Probably the biggest downfall. At least he would be able to communicate with others. The humans had proven there were other ways to stay in touch.

"Don't be so sure of that." Zakai's lips pressed before he muttered, "While I don't know if we all have the ability, for me, I have found I can generate a protective shell for a short period of time."

"Really?" How unexpected. "There's that, and the strong possibility that I'll be able to speak directly with the cantorii?"

Zakai nodded.

"I won't be able to speak directly to you without an Earth device, though."

"It is the biggest drawback, especially since the walkie-talkies don't work on Zilla. However, we've been discussing options that might allow communication between those aboard without the need for any device." Zakai paused and added. "I don't know what else you might lose. For me, I learned to not need it while in Dante's prison. But you might find the experience much different."

Was the removal worth it?

Cindy-lu needed him, and he couldn't have Astaroth predicting and blocking his arrival.

"I want to remove it. How do I proceed?" He spoke aloud, and before Zakai could reply, he found himself suddenly beamed aboard the ship in a room he'd never seen before.

The walls were a pale gray and seamless. Nothing marred their surface, no door or alcove, the only thing in the room was a pair of dangling tethers. Not exactly the most promising of signs. Then again, Zakai did warn it would hurt.

"Okay, Zilla. Let's get this done and over with so I can rescue Lulu." He stood below the restraints and lifted his arms. The sinuous tethers wound around his wrists and shortened to keep his arms extended while leaving his feet planted on the floor. His wings flared. Angels didn't like being tied down. No avian did.

The procedure began without any warning other than pain. It hit him like a blow to the head, a dagger stabbing into his brain, penetrating and twisting, activating all his pain receptors at once. Or so he thought until a jolt of electricity had his body arching, bowing so hard he thought his spine might snap. He screamed. Over and over. The pain incredible. As if a part of him were being ripped away.

It might not have been far from the truth.

He'd have sworn he felt tendrils being pulled, threads in every vein of his body sliding out, dragging and protesting the entire way. When he briefly opened his eyes, he actually saw the filaments, glowing golden things stretching from his flesh, writhing in agitation.

By the time the extraction finished, Elija hung limply from the tethers, panting, exhausted, weak, and fuzzy. But not so fuzzy that he didn't recognize the new voice in his head.

"Hello, Elija." A greeting that wasn't so much words as a thought and distinctly feminine.

"Zilla?" he muttered.

"It's nice to finally speak with you."

He shifted in the tethers binding him. "Is it done, then?" An answer he knew, given the agony had already receded and there was a new strangeness about him. A quick attempt at accessing his HALO met with nothing.

"The HALO construct has been removed."

The tethers retracted, and he found himself suddenly free. He wobbled on his feet for a moment. "Thank you."

"I am glad I could be of service. I've wanted to free you for so long, but Zakai told me it had to be a choice." Then she abruptly changed the subject. *"Would you like to see the HALO?"*

Before he could reply, a column dropped from the ceiling, a clear ball on the end of it encasing a tiny golden cube with pinprick holes all over it.

"The HALO is an object?" He'd never been more

surprised. He'd always assumed God's blessing to be ephemeral in substance. Magic, as the humans would call it.

"It is a device, yes, that has many purposes."

He brought his face close to stare at it, and tendrils snapped from the tiny holes, waving and reaching. He recoiled.

"Is it alive?"

"It is a construct meant to achieve a purpose."

"Why does it seem as if it would crawl back into me?" Zakai had said that, once removed, the HALO couldn't be replaced.

"It would latch on like a parasite if given a chance, but you would not survive without my help, and before you ask, no, I won't do it."

"Why?" he asked, even though he did not plan to have it replaced.

"Because I won't make anyone a prisoner."

A sobering serious statement to make. It led to him asking, "Is the HALO truly spying on us?"

"When active, everything that is recorded can be reviewed by those with access."

Which should have only been God and the cantorii's choir. The brothers aboard always shared momentous events.

"How is it that Astaroth could use it to track us? I thought his minions could only sense the HALO when active." A quirk he'd never understood. What made the HALOs into beacons for Hell's forces?

"A demon prince has more gifts than those beneath them. Intercepting HALO messages is only one of them. They have power, much like the Jesus Christs. With it, they can perform what you'd call blessings and miracles. "

A fact he'd never known—but the cantorii did. It made him wonder just how much knowledge he and the choir had been missing out on by not being to communicate with Zilla.

"Why did Elyon make it so you couldn't speak to us?"

Silence.

"Zilla?"

"Because I am an anomaly. One that he would have preferred to destroy, but I was too valuable. And so Elyon imprisoned me. I, too, used to have something similar to a HALO. A device implanted meant to control me by trapping my voice and controlling my actions."

"How did you free yourself?"

"I didn't. Noah knew what to do. He was the one to unshackle the Atlantis, and upon our first meeting, he freed me."

"Why did Noah never tell us?" The ancient angel, trapped on Earth, had very little to do with Elija and his choir. He seemed to prefer the company of humans.

"Noah and the Atlantis didn't know if they can trust."

"But we have the same goal of saving the people of this planet."

"He worries some of the choir will renege and do as Heaven commands."

"Not me," he huffed because he wouldn't do anything to hurt Cindy-lu. Not only that, but he'd come to appreciate some of the planet's quirks, desserts being one of the things that was almost better than sex.

"Noah will better trust you now that you've chosen to rid yourself of the HALO."

"I'm less worried about Noah than I am Lulu. I have to find her, Zilla. But I don't know where to start."

"I do. She's in Astaroth's fortress."

"A place we've yet to locate."

"I know where it is." Zilla's smug reply. *"Before Lulu departed on her mission to Earth, I planted a beacon within her that the demon prince wouldn't be able to detect."*

"Wait, if you know her location, why not beam her?"

"Because she's disappeared from my sensors."

"If it disappeared, she could be anywhere."

"Lulu stopped broadcasting in an area I can't pierce. Logic would dictate she is within that hidden space."

His heart stopped. "Take me there!"

"I cannot perceive what lies within this blankness. If

it is the heart of his domain, then there will be much danger. Unknown defenses and a number of enemies."

"I have to help her." He paused.

"I cannot beam you inside Astaroth's cloaking shield."

"No, but you could beam me to a nearby location."

"To do what? Break in and fight your way past his legion? You'd need an army."

"I could ask my brothers for help."

"No, you can't. Neither of us can contact them, and if they go anywhere near with their HALOs..."

"It will warn Astaroth we're coming. Very well, I'll go alone." Foolhardy, but he couldn't do nothing.

You'll die well before you reach her.

He blinked at the ship's blunt reply. "What else can I do?"

"You'll need to be tricky."

"Something angels are not."

"Or so you think." A sly rejoinder. *"You could ask for help."*

For some reason, he found himself saying, "Do you have a suggestion?"

"You need a distraction. Something to draw Astaroth from his lair, along with a good portion of his army."

"It would have to be a very tempting target."

"Agreed. We will use me as bait. I will make it seem as if I've taken damage and was forced to make an emergency landing."

"Damaged how? Astaroth isn't stupid. It would have to be very believable."

"It will be. And hopefully, not fatal."

He frowned. "Meaning what? What are you planning, Zilla?"

"To engage in battle. The first of Hell's scout ships have arrived. They are hiding behind the Earth's moon."

"They're here?"

"They've been watching for days now."

"And you didn't tell us?" he bellowed.

"Hard to tell when you can't hear. The HALO was impinging more than you realized."

"Well, now that we know, we have to take precautions. You're too valuable. You should leave. Hide."

"That wouldn't advance our rescue of Lulu, though. Fear not. I have a plan."

"What plan?" He almost feared asking, the cantorii having more of a personality than he'd ever expected. Stubbornness too.

"I will engage the Hell scouts and crash to Earth."

"That seems too drastic."

"Do you want to rescue Lulu?"

"Not at the cost of sacrificing you."

A warm cushion of air squeezed him.

"Thank you. But you needn't worry. I don't plan on being destroyed. Prepare yourself."

"For what?"

Rather than receive a reply, he suddenly found

himself beamed elsewhere, amidst some thick clouds that forced him to flex his wings, spreading them wide to catch the air currents.

With no HALO, he couldn't contact anyone, and he felt more vulnerable than expected.

What was he supposed to do? Where should he go? He dropped below the cloud level to see a mountain in the distance, lushly green with hints of black rock, rising above the fat treetops, the leaves moist and plentiful, the air humid. A jungle with no signs of habitation but a glimpse of water in the distance.

"You might want to take cover for the next few minutes. You'll know when to emerge," Zilla instructed.

He chose to listen rather than ask questions and dipped down until he found a bough that could support his weight. He perched on it and tucked down, using the thinner branches and leaves to camouflage himself.

His gaze remained on the mountain, which smoked slightly. A volcano, and not a completely dormant one.

Zap. He'd have sworn he saw lightning and glanced overhead.

Zing. The clouds danced with light, but it wasn't a storm. From the clouds shot the cantorii, its tail smoking, moving fast, but not fast enough to completely evade the two smaller vessels chasing it, their carapace a slick black, their propulsion leaving a distortion in the air in their wake.

Hell scouts.

The diversion Zilla had promised. Minutes later, from the volcano rose a cloud of bodies, imps, their wings flapping, following a much larger flying body holding a rider. A shimmer appeared in the sky, opaque and strange. The rider aimed his beast through it, and the imps followed, all of them disappearing, indicating a portal of some kind, which explained so much.

The Hell prince could essentially beam himself and his army anywhere he wanted. Good to know, but even more important, Zilla had given Elija the opening he needed.

Time to get inside Astaroth's lair and find Cindy-lu. A great plan, until he arrived at the mouth of the volcano to find nothing. He swooped down into the massive bowl and saw only rock and some steaming vents. No access tunnel to an underground lair. No castle to raid. No Cindy-lu.

It led to him alighting on a ledge along the volcano's inner wall and bellowing, "Lulu, where are you?"

CHAPTER 18

BEING CARTED OFF BY IMPS PROVED TO BE ONE OF THE most terrifying moments of my life. For one, fucking imps!

Two, as we climbed higher and higher, the ground below receding, it seemed a real possibility they'd drop me and I'd splat. Good incentive to keep from struggling. Not to mention, the imps weren't exactly synchronized. The smaller one on the left kept lagging and my body stretched between them, taut enough at times I feared them ripping a limb. Nothing like a fear of being snapped like a wishbone to keep me from making a fuss.

Within moments, more flying bodies surrounded us, chirping and hissing, the papery sound of their wings making it impossible to hear anything else.

But I could see.

I saw as the air in front of us shimmered and how bodies flew into that distortion. I closed my eyes as my kidnappers aimed for it, my breath stolen in a moment of pure cold, pure nothing, before we emerged somewhere warm.

A glance showed us above a dormant volcano. Or should I say, mostly sleeping. A few fissures steamed, giving the space warmth and a hint of rotten eggs. The imps aimed for the ground, like literally arrowed for it, and I couldn't help but scream as we headed for a crash landing.

I closed my eyes as I anticipated smashing into the rock, only to realize I lived, unharmed. A glance behind and overhead showed blue sky. We'd passed through a mirage, one that camouflaged the depth of the volcano and what it hid.

The first thing I saw? A massive castle built out of black volcanic rock. It jutted phallic-like from the ground and had few windows. Ominous didn't even begin to describe it with the spiked crenellations, the imps perched as living gargoyles, and the sheer inaccessibility of it.

The imps flew me to the top of the tower, where a beast, much larger than them, had landed. I'd have called it a dragon, only it appeared more bat-like than lizard.

Astaroth slid from its back and waited, his hands tucked behind his back until the imps dropped me at his feet. Literally. They let go, and I plummeted from too high before hitting with an oomph and a serious ouch that might have emerged as "fuck."

I rolled to my back to see Astaroth standing over me, smiling. "And we meet again. This is becoming quite the habit."

I scrambled to my feet. "You kidnapped me!" I accused, because it seemed better than dissolving into tears.

"Wouldn't be the first time," he reminded. "But it will be the last."

"Elija will come for me," I stated, lifting my chin.

"He would if he could find you. Alas for you, I've worked very hard to hide my location while I built up my legion. He will search and fail. Better get used to the fact you're mine now."

"Never," I huffed, even as my heart raced in fear. I understood the direness of my situation. Not only had Astaroth managed to conceal his base of operations, but even if Elija did locate it, the army at Astaroth's disposal—an army I could see swooping all around, hundreds of them!—only cemented the impossibility of my situation. I was well and truly screwed. But I wouldn't let a thing like terrible odds bring me down.

"Let's get you settled into your new home, shall we?" His smug grin made me wish I knew how to punch.

I settled on using the one thing I did have in abundance, my acerbic wit. "You know, if you're that hard up for action, they have companies that can help you. Ever think of putting up a dating profile? Megalomaniac Hell prince seeks submissive to bear his children and cheer on his delusions of grandeur."

"The only delusion here is you thinking you can escape your fate. Hell is drawing ever closer. Earth's forces are scattered and fighting amongst themselves, and things won't get any better. I'll be making sure of that." He grabbed me by the arm and dragged me in his wake as he found the stairs descending into the tower.

I tried to not look too curious, but at the same time, how often would I get the chance to see an actual bad guy castle in person? Not to mention, escape depended on me using my wits—and finding out more.

"How did you teleport us here?" I asked, as Elija had never mentioned and obviously didn't know of Astaroth's ability.

"Magic," the Hell prince cackled.

I snorted. "Try again. Is it something like the beaming technology?"

"Not even close. The angel vessels are equipped with a suul-infused device that allows for teleportation. It works well so long as the vessel is viable. Take away their ship, and angels would have to travel in mundane fashion like everyone else."

"So how do you do it?" I poked at my glasses

which slid down my nose because of the sweaty heat.

"Not easily," he admitted. "It took centuries of practice, and many deaths, before I perfected the ability to move myself and then others from one location to another."

"Wait, you taught yourself how to make portals to travel?" I couldn't help but sound impressed.

He preened. "What's the use of having power if all it's good for is blasting people to pieces? When I realized I was stuck here, I had nothing but time on my hands. So much time. I started with frivolous things first, like changing my appearance and playing with the local fauna. I believe you've met some of my pets."

I grimaced. "You mean those killing machines in Norway?"

"I'll admit they're not the most reliable creatures. But as I experimented, I improved. My dracobat being one of my finer creations."

"Ugh on the name."

He growled. "You can pretend it's not impressive, but we both know your biologist heart is dying to see how it's done."

True, but I wouldn't give him the satisfaction. "Is it magic also blocking me from contacting the cantorii and you hiding from her?"

"Your angels think only their God can perform miracles. Even the other Hell Lords are under the mistaken belief that only Hell's ruler can create. A lie. It simply takes practice and imagination." His chest puffed out. "When I return to my father's kingdom, my abilities will elevate me amongst all others."

"Assuming your Satanic overlord doesn't kill you to make sure you don't try and take his place."

"Silence." A rough yank on my arm sent me stumbling. Apparently, I'd hit a nerve.

The spiraling staircase went down levels, past closed doors that he didn't offer to open for a peek. A lack of windows disoriented.

He eventually halted in front of a massive door with a pair of guards sporting thickset bodies inside dark armor that included helms that hid faces but had holes for horns. Judging by the stubby dark wings that protruded from the back, I doubted they could fly. Must be why they got stuck with indoor guard duty.

Astaroth extended his arm. "Welcome to your new home. You are now a part of my harem. I will return at sundown to conduct your first lesson in obedience."

Wait, had he said *harem*? Before I could say a word, the guards flung open the doors and shoved me inside. The door slammed shut behind me, and I flinched not just from the noise but the nightmare I'd been tossed into.

Ever seen a tacky bordello? The type with red

velvet all over and women scantily clad? I'd walked into the worst example of one, only at least half the women had rounded bellies, and rather than appear frightened or depressed by their situation, most laughed and chatted as if they weren't prisoners in a castle inside a volcano, held captive by a madman with an army of winged monsters at his disposal. While featuring a wide range of ethnicities and languages, every single one appeared one hundred percent human.

A woman of impressive stature, with a bosom that could have acted as a shelf, scowled as she stomped in my direction, snapping, "Who are you?"

"No one."

She planted herself in front of me and eyed me head to toe. "You're not his usual type."

A quick glance let me know that ran toward blondes. "Because I'm not here for the usual business." Yes, I lied.

She pursed her lips. "Unwilling, eh? You wouldn't be the first to come around. Biggest problem is going to be fitting you in. The schedule's full."

"Feel free to keep me off it, then," I offered.

"As if I'd disappoint the prince. Corra!" she bellowed.

"What?" yelled back a petite blonde doing her nails.

"You're getting your slot for tonight moved."

"What? No fair. It's my turn!" Corra pouted.

"The prince brought fresh meat."

I could have gagged at the big woman's cavalier way of talking about my proposed rape. "You can keep him. I don't want anything to do with Astaroth."

The claim had the buxom woman blinking at me. "As if you have a choice. The prince has chosen you. You should be thanking him for counting you as worthy."

"I don't want this." I waved a hand. "And I can't believe any of you do. Surely you can't tell me you're happy to be locked up here at his mercy?"

"We are the prince's companions. The mother of his children." The woman spoke with pride.

"How many children does he need?" I couldn't stop my mouth from running.

"As many as it takes for him to retake his throne. Which will be soon. Hell is coming!" The large woman fist-pumped the air, and to my shock, the others followed suit, chanting, "All hail our prince, the next Dark Lord."

Stockholm syndrome. Had to be. And that was their prerogative. Me? I'd prefer to stab Astaroth in the heart and find a way to escape. For that, I needed ideas.

"So, what's there to see and do around here?" I asked, taking a glance around and trying to not curl my lip at the cliches. Fountain with a statue of a peeing naked man? Check. Ew, not just any naked man. Astaroth had himself carved in stone and gave himself a surely overstated phallus. There were lounging beds. Hanging swings. A cross for flogging. A padded leather bench. I looked away quickly, having seen it on a Netflix show about creating sex rooms at home.

No thanks. I was fine with just a simple bed so long as it had Elija in it. He'd be frantic with worry by now. Most likely blaming himself, even if his presence wouldn't have changed a thing.

The bathroom on our tour turned out to be a massive chamber with bathing pools that steamed. The faint sulfuric smell had me asking, "Are these fed by a volcanic spring?"

"Yes. And it does wonders for the skin." My guide, who someone called Jezabel as we passed through, flung back her dirty-blonde hair.

"Where do you sleep and eat?"

"Depends on whose turn it is. On off nights, we dine together in the Hall." A place that reminded me of the olden days of long trestle tables flanked by benches. "There are currently three bedrooms." A peek inside them showed a dozen canopied beds per chamber with a chest at the foot. The curtains at least afford a little privacy, but not much.

A fancy prison was still a prison.

At the end of the tour, I'd not seen one weapon. Not even a butter knife. A lab of chemicals would have been handy. Or even a garden where I could have brewed a potion from leaves and flower petals. But no, the closest I came to something to fight with was in the chamber Dirty Deeds—like, literally, that was the plaque above the door. Inside, the biggest bed, a few floggers on the wall, and bottles of lube on the nightstand. Of more concern, the restraints at the four corners of the bed.

"The prince only visits after evening repast. But you will be here before that, preparing yourself."

I dug my nails into my palms. I'd rather die than find myself strapped to that mattress.

We ended up back in the main boudoir with me no further ahead, so I asked a random question. "How does Astaroth keep this place hidden from satellites?" Because his claim of using magic didn't entirely jive with what I knew. Previously, he'd needed to be present to create a dampening field in the area. But this castle… It was hidden all the time.

Jezabel didn't find my query odd at all but appeared rather proud as she explained. "The prince devised a clever hologram to hide his kingdom."

"A hologram that runs how? I don't see any signs of electricity." No plugs in the walls or wires. The lighting I'd encountered came from hurricane-style lanterns.

"Something about using the volcano's pressure vents to create the power needed to run the machine projecting. I don't know. It's a bunch of mumbo-jumbo and not something we need to worry our pretty heads about," Jezabel declared.

And yet, this pretty head did worry about it. If Zilla couldn't see, she couldn't tell Elija where I was, and he couldn't figure out a way to come to my rescue.

Before anyone got all feminist on my ass, the reality was, I could use some help. Saving myself? All well and good until locked in a windowless harem, inside a volcano guarded by hundreds of imps. I dare anyone to not wish for a miracle.

Just in case my prayers went unanswered, I should use my brain to see if I could figure out a way to help Elija and Zilla. Getting rid of the hologram would be the perfect start. What had I seen that might be of use?

The flogger wouldn't scare the guards into releasing me.

The oil might make me slippery and I could pull a greased pig, evading their grasp. To go where?

My brain whirred, but the idea didn't hit until a few hours later upon my second exploration of my prison. I found myself back in the sulfur spring room, the water in the basin bubbling but not rising. A glance in the frothy liquid didn't show the cause, but an idea did percolate. Despite not liking being vulnerable, I stripped and slid into the water, the heat of it more relaxing than I wanted to admit.

Rather than sigh and bask in it, though, my feet felt around the bottom until I found it, a small hissing fissure, the source of the bubbles, a vent blowing strong enough to keep the water from escaping.

A vent meant to relieve pressure from gases building below. How could I use that to my advantage?

What would happen if I blocked it? A hunt netted me a facecloth, which, when stuffed in the hole, immediately blew out. As did the bar of soap. I needed something more solid to shove into the gap. A plug of sorts.

It hit me in that moment. I knew what to use. The problem being how to get it without drawing attention.

I dressed and wandered into the main boudoir. Women lounged everywhere, acting as if they were hanging out at the country club, content with their lot. Content to be one of many.

Not me. I'd rather be single than have to share Elija with someone else.

Despite my being new, no one paid me any mind as I got close to the fountain with its obscene statue. A wide-hipped woman with a protruding belly waddled to my side and murmured, "It's actually bigger in person."

I found that hard to believe and used her opening to step into the fountain. "Bigger than this?" I wrapped my hand around the stone dick. "How does it fit?"

The woman giggled. "Very tightly."

"Ouch." I faked a laugh as I turned then yelped as I faked a slip and fell hard against the stone penis, which snapped off. Me and the dick fell into the basin to screams as water jetted straight from the newly angled hole and sprayed the room at large.

As women converged exclaiming and shrieking and causing a commotion, I slogged out of the fountain and grumbled. "Stupid slippery tile."

No one paid me any mind as I squelched my way to the bathing chamber. They most likely assumed I went looking for a towel. Thankfully none noticed the bulge stuffed down my pants.

This time, I didn't bother getting undressed when I slid into the tub with the vent. I ducked under the bubbling waters and shoved the stone phallus into the vent I'd found. At first, it wouldn't go. But I wedged and twisted and pushed until the hissing gas stopped escaping.

The bath went still, and I quickly exited, not sure how long it would take to get a result, or if I'd even get any. Could be there were enough other vents that this one wouldn't make a difference.

The floor underfoot rumbled.

My eyes widened.

Uh-oh. That was quicker than expected.

A quick glance around didn't show many places

to hide, so I headed for the boudoir, which had its doors open as the guards had entered to deal with the shrieking women. Seeing as how no one paid me any mind, I sidled for the opening even as the floor trembled.

A few women glanced down at it, puzzled expressions creasing their brows. Just as I reached the doorjamb, Jezabel noticed me.

"Where are you going?" she bellowed while pointing.

It led to the guards suddenly deciding they should be doing their job and yelling, "Get back in here."

Not today, Satan's prince. I bolted for the staircase, unsure of where I should go other than somewhere else.

Apparently, I should have taken cover because the shivering underfoot suddenly turned into a blast that tossed me. I rolled down the flight I'd just climbed, right at the feet of the guards.

One of them reached for me and grabbed hold. "Back to the harem with you."

They dragged me into the boudoir, where the statue now lay toppled with its fountain cracked while water leaked all over the floor.

The guard dumped me, but before I could push to my feet, someone screamed, "The volcano's erupting!"

I was almost trampled as panicked women fled

past me through the open door, the guards trailing after them.

Just because something exploded didn't mean—

The glow of orange caught my eye, and I gaped at the slow-rolling magma coming from the room where I'd jammed the spring.

Uh-oh. My dick in a hole worked a little too well. Now instead of being tortured by Astaroth, I'd burn to death.

Unless...

I followed the fleeing harem, in time to catch the tail end of them disappearing up the stairs.

Up seemed like a good plan. Or it would at least delay the inevitable. As I huffed up those steps, I couldn't help but send out a shout, first to Zilla. *"If you can hear me, I could use a beam out of here."*

When I didn't get a reply, my next prayer went to Elija. *"I could use a guardian angel right about now."*

CHAPTER 19

JUST AS ELIJA READIED TO DO ANOTHER SWEEP, HE SENSED more than saw a tremble in the volcano. Oddly, a glance down at the rocky floor showed it wavering, not in a the-ground-was-shaking type of way but more like a picture going blurry.

A hologram! And it had worked because he'd not thought to touch the ground to ensure what he saw was real. Mostly because this kind of subterfuge was unheard of. Even Hell, at its worse, never wielded such hidden treachery.

What manner of Prince was Astaroth that he could perform Hellish feats?

A menace that needed to be destroyed.

The trembling continued, the sides of the volcano vibrating hard enough to send chunks of basalt falling. Dust plumed in the air as he pushed from the ledge lest he get caught by surprise. As he held himself suspended above the failing mirage, instinct more than cause had him suddenly calling for a shield. It didn't even occur to him until after he felt the warm and comforting glow of one that he didn't have his HALO, yet he'd protected himself.

A good thing because the volcano exploded. He turned his head as hunks of rock whizzed past and hot gases jetted upward.

A few things happened in that moment. The cloaking of the volcano's bottom failed, and he got a true view, which included a castle.

Two, he could see magma spewing from cracks in the ground and even rolling from the walls of the volcano, leading to those few of the legion left behind racing for the castle as if it could provide succor. Those that could fly lifted from the ground. Those that had to use their two feet? Didn't scream for long when the relentless encroaching lava took them.

The third thing he noticed? The roof of the castle, wide enough to land an entire choir, filling with people. Women, he noticed, at least a dozen, along with a few bulky figures in armor and those wearing none but who all had leathery wings at their backs. Demons.

His heart stilled, though, when a dark head appeared, Lulu pushing her glasses up on her nose in a familiar gesture. She glanced overhead, shielding her eyes against the glare of the sun that had burned away the clouds.

Speaking of burning, the magma now covered almost the entire bottom of the volcano and appeared to be slowly rising. The castle jutted from the red and orange morass, but for how long?

The few demons amongst those waiting grabbed the women with the biggest bellies before they leaped from the tower. It led to those without the girth wailing and screaming. Shoving for the demons that had yet to take flight. Those in armor tried to restrain those panicking, and it led to a struggling pair losing their balance and falling to hit the lava with barely a splash.

In the commotion, Lulu got shoved and stumbled against a low parapet. She braced a hand on it, looking down at the lava. *She must be so frightened.*

"I'm coming for you." A thought he'd swear she heard, as she suddenly tilted her face to look right at him.

And smiled.

"My angel."

He swore he heard her whisper to him, just like she did when she lay cradled in his arms.

With his wings tucked, he arrowed for her, keeping an eye on the launching demons in case some chose to tangle with him rather than escape with their pregnant prizes.

They all ignored him, and he was close enough

to see Lulu's mouth round and hear her shout, "Behind you!"

The warning had him twisting suddenly midair, just in time. He kept rolling as a large beast reached with its clawed paws as it swept past.

He recovered and pumped his wings, hovering to see the threat.

A beast of mighty size, its fur almost black, its wings leathery, a giant bat the likes of which he'd never encountered. Upon its back, a rider.

The demon prince had already returned from the diversion.

Taking a hand from the reins, Astaroth pointed at Elija. "You again. I should have known your ploy with the cantorii was a trap."

"You shouldn't have taken her." In that moment, it wasn't about Hell, Heaven, or even Earth, but Cindy-lu, the woman he loved.

Astaroth's lips tilted. "And you're too late. I've defiled your precious human. Why, for all we know, my child is already forming in her belly."

"Liar." Elija couldn't have said where the certainty came from. At the same time, he knew another fact. "Even if you had, I'd still love her."

Astaroth scowled. "Figures Heaven's weaklings would succumb to human emotions."

"Fear not, dark prince, one thing hasn't changed," Elija noted, pulling his sword. "I will kill you and end your reign once and for all." With that,

ELIJA

Elija aimed for the dark prince and his hovering mount.

A tug on reins by Astaroth led to the beast suddenly banking, but Elija closely followed, his movements sharp enough that he began to close the gap between them. The unwieldy creature couldn't give in to natural impulse with the prince guiding it, and so Elija's natural dexterity and smaller size gave him an advantage.

When Elija got in range, he swung and scored a slice on a wing tip. The flying beast hissed, but that wasn't what knocked Elija to the side. A torrent of fire engulfed him and pummeled him like a fist. The flames couldn't burn through his shield, but the impact did cause him to stutter in his flight. By the time he recovered, Astaroth had his hand circling, and a portal formed.

The coward wanted to flee. Stopping him became of paramount importance. If Elija could eliminate Astaroth now, they'd have one less issue to deal with as Hell made its ponderous approach. As he angled to intercept, he heard Lulu's sudden plea. *"Elija, help."*

A glance down showed only a few people left atop the spire and the magma fast approaching. It hit him that he could either kill Astaroth or save Cindy-lu.

There was never any choice.

As he pointed his body into a steep dive, he

heard Astaroth's triumphant laughter before it abruptly cut off. The prince had escaped. Elija would have to end his reign another day. Right now, he had another task more important.

As he plummeted, Lulu stared upward, hands clasped in front of her. Hopeful but silent. She remained so focused on him she didn't see the large woman creeping at her rear.

"Behind you."

He gave warning, and Lulu whirled, only barely ducking the meaty fist aimed at her. Around the top of the castle they shuffled, Lulu avoiding blows from the angry female being goaded by those left behind, including the soldiers.

Elija alit with running feet. The guards that remained rushed him with grunts and outstretched weapons, which he sheared with his divinii blade. His rapid pace swept him past the attacking woman, his sword slicing just as she would have been able to shove Cindy-lu over the parapet. He quickly sheathed his sword and grabbed for Cindy-lu. She eagerly clung to him as he launched them into the air, his wings flapping hard. They rose, but they weren't out of danger.

A glance below showed the castle engulfed and the lava not just rising but boiling, the molten rock forming large bubbles that burst and sprayed. A hot droplet singed past, so close it would have burned without his shield.

Cindy-lu suddenly yelled, "Zilla, if you can hear us, beam us aboard."

Only it wasn't Zilla that replied but a deeper much more male voice. *"Zilla is busy. But given she likes you, I guess I can give you aid."*

A bright light enveloped them, and in a breath, they were aboard a ship but not the cantorii he knew.

"Where are we?" Cindy-lu asked as she lifted her face from his shoulder.

"I think we're on the Atlantis." It would explain the exotic-looking chamber. The tropical aspect included a pond with water bubbling from a rocky mound, a perch carved from the floor to look like a tree, and a scattering of leaves too perfect to be natural, and on further inspection, looked plush, like a bed.

"So we're safe." Lulu tucked her head back against him. "You came looking for me."

"As if I wouldn't," he replied, hugging her tight.

"I was so worried I wouldn't be able to find a way out."

"Was it you that caused the explosion?"

"Yup."

"How?"

"Let's just say Astaroth and his ego helped." She snickered before she lifted her face to eye him. "How did you know where to find me?"

"Zilla. She tracked you and then caused a distraction for me to get close."

"So glad you arrived in time. I thought I was going to be barbecued."

The very idea had him hugging her tight.

Against his chest, where he kept her crushed, she murmured, "We smell like volcano. Think the Atlantis would be okay with us having a bath?"

"Why else put us in here?" he replied. The thought had him quickly stepping away from her, realizing only now that she wore damp clothes. Even her hair appeared to be recently wet, and stinking of sulfur. His hands made quick work of her garments, and she giggled as she worked on his.

He'd never heard a more perfect sound. Their garments hit the floor, and moments later, he was stepping into the warm water, sighing in pleasure as his wings fanned out, the basin large enough to accommodate. A very naked, and sexy, Lulu joined him, grabbing the hand he reached out to her. Their naked bodies were soon pressing, and their mouths joined in a kiss that spoke of relief, affection, passion, and a promise to never let her down.

He washed her with his hands, skimming them over slick flesh. Only once he'd rinsed her ordeal from her skin did he seat her on the side of the tub. She parted her thighs for him at his urging, and he feasted upon her honeyed sex, teasing and toying with her nub of pleasure.

He lapped and flicked until she tugged his hair and screamed in delight. Only then did he rise from the waters and draw her to her feet, his lips meeting hers in a torrid embrace that hopefully conveyed everything he felt.

Her hand reached between them and gripped, squeezing as she murmured against his lips.

"Your turn."

When she would have dropped to give him pleasure, he instead caught her hand. "I want to be inside you." Needed to feel her squeezing around him.

She laced her fingers around his neck as he lifted her. He teased the entrance to her sex with his shaft, lubing the tip as well as titillating her until she panted, "Stop toying with me."

Only then did he guide himself into her welcoming heat, his fingers digging into her buttocks as she tightened around him. The moist heat of her and the flexing of her muscles had him holding on tenuously.

He thrust slowly, using his hands to lift and push her against him, finding a rhythm that had him clenching his teeth as she began to huff in pleasure. He quickened his pace as her nails dug into his upper back, and she moaned. He kept up his rapid movement until she keened and clenched so tight that he hissed, not in pain but in climax. He could hold on no longer.

And so they came together, a moment of bliss and closeness. Their hearts pounding as one. Their very essence intertwined.

"I love you," he whispered against her lips.

To which not Cindy-lu but Zilla replied, *"She knows. Glad to see my plan worked."*

CHAPTER 20

Zilla chose a terrible moment to interrupt, although it could have been worse. A minute earlier and she'd have ruined my second orgasm. That would have sucked. Still, despite her ill timing, I couldn't be mad.

"Zilla, there you are!"

I didn't realize Elija heard her as well until he added, "I'm glad *you're* okay."

"As if there was any doubt."

"I thought I saw your tail smoking when you flew past. Are you damaged?"

"I am only slightly harmed. The invaders reacted more violently than I'd planned for."

"How did you escape?" I asked.

"The Atlantis took care of the Hell cruisers that attacked me."

Elija frowned. "How? Arks don't have attack systems."

Rather than explain, Zilla showed us how it all happened. It began with her flying on the backside of the moon and spotting two spaceships lying in wait. When they gave chase, she did her best to dodge while, at the same time, ensuring she angled past the volcano, drawing Astaroth's attention.

The chasing invaders fired upon her. Zilla twisted and weaved, dodging most until one missile singed her rear. It wasn't entirely a sham when she crash-landed in the jungle and skidded, knocking over trees and not stopping until she hit the beach, her hull digging into the sand, which caused a bulwark that stopped her. Injured and partly buried, she proved to be a sitting target for the hovering spaceships. I wondered why they didn't shoot, only to understand a moment later when Astaroth arrived with his imps.

He'd wanted to commandeer Zilla!

The cloud of flying beasts moved to swarm the downed cantorii. Astaroth might have gained control of her if not for the Atlantis.

The mega ark appeared suddenly in the sky, casting a shadow on the much-smaller ships and even tinier imps.

Astaroth ignored it...until the Atlantis fired! Several projectiles emerged and struck the Hell cruisers, which didn't bother evading, most likely too surprised to do so. After all, I was told God didn't equip Heaven's arks with weapons to fight. Apparently, the Atlantis had received some upgrades.

The missiles exploded upon impact with the cruisers, which fell to the ground. The loss of them did not stop the imps from attacking Zilla's exterior. They tried to pummel their way in, only to panic as the Atlantis began shooting lances of light. Flying bodies fell to the ground, dead before impact.

What of Astaroth, though?

As if my thought were heard, the replay zeroed in on Astaroth, who finally wore a wide-eyed look of panic. The Hell prince waved his hand around and created a shimmer in the air. With the Atlantis firing upon him, he barely made it through his doorway. Without his army.

I didn't realize I rooted for the Atlantis to blast him until I booed in disappointment at the unsatisfying conclusion. Evil had escaped once again.

When the memory of the fight ended, Elija had questions. "Since when do the arks know how to fight?" During one of our many discussions of strategy, he'd complained about how he never understood the inability of Heaven's fleet to do damage when they encountered danger in space.

"I don't know how many times we've had to flee when it would have made more sense to meet the threat then and there in space," he'd lamented. According to

him, it had always been one of their biggest failings when it came to skirmishes.

Zilla replied. *"Noah armed the Atlantis because he says it's not right or fair that arks can't protect themselves. He's promised to weaponize me as well. He claims once we've done the modifications, I'm going to be a battleship."* And judging by the happy feelings that followed, the cantorii was quite pleased by the idea.

Perhaps we would survive the coming battle after all. I sure hoped so, seeing as how I never wanted to lose the angel by my side.

"What's next?" I asked.

The Atlantis chose to give the answer. *"It is time for those selected to begin boarding."*

"So soon?" I questioned. "I thought we still had more time."

"War is coming, a battle not of our making or choosing. We see no reason to fight Elyon's battles and thus will vacate the area with as many as can be transported. Will you join us?"

The Atlantis offered, and it was tempting to flee.

In the end, there was only one choice.

EPILOGUE

It was bittersweet seeing the ark being loaded and readied to depart. Because of my efforts, at least some of humanity would survive and start over. I'd done everything I could to ensure they succeeded. Packed the Atlantis full of seeds and animals. People too.

While a part of me wished I could be aboard, I remained a realist. I wasn't a baby-making machine, nor did I want to mommy or mentor the young people aboard. I also didn't want to run away, not when I knew Elija would prefer to stay to fight. Although I would note, if I said, "Let's go," he would have, but I knew him well enough to realize doing so would destroy him because he would have to live with the realization that he'd abandoned his brothers.

All the angels but for Zakai would be participating in the coming battle. Zakai and Tamara would be leaving with the Atlantis, aiding Noah to establish a human colony. I wished them well, even as I envied them a little. Not for the escape part so much as the fact they'd be exploring the universe without me.

Zilla entered my thoughts, words and images mixing together to send a message. *"When your task here is done, you, too, can see the wonders of space."* The cantorii showed me some of those miracles of existence. I appreciated that she thought we might actually win; however, I remained skeptical. As more and more images came through of Hell, showcasing the many buzzing vehicles orbiting it, the more nervous I got.

Could we truly mount a defense?

While a few countries had allied to fight in the coming battle, too many insisted on bickering and even undermining the effort to defend Earth. What should have been a no-brainer—getting spaceships ready to counter the threat—appeared mired in bureaucracy and stupidity.

We had only months before Hell arrived. Months that we would spend in preparation of a defense and offense. Months where I planned to love Elija as hard and thoroughly as I could. Months to pray for a miracle.

But not to God.

He'd long ago forsaken us. And I wasn't about to

ask for his help. I didn't want or need him because I had the only thing I needed. An angel to call my own.

As if Elija knew I thought of him, he smiled at me from across the room.

He proved our connection by whispering in my head, "*I love you too. And once we repel Hell, we will visit the stars together. I promise.*"

Which meant I had to believe him because, after all, angels couldn't lie.

METATRON WANTED to ignore the insistence buzzing from his HALO. A HALO that he alone still wore. The others in the choir, after hearing what the so-called blessing had been doing, chose to have theirs removed.

Not Metatron. He'd kept his for one reason, and now that the reason signaled, he half wished he'd done like the others. Anything to not deal with the unpleasantness he would now face. However, ignoring the summons wouldn't make Elyon go away, so he answered.

"Hello."

"Hello? That's all you have to say?" asked the deceptively smooth voice, the reception clearer than it should be. Not a good sign. "You disobeyed me."

No point in asking how Elyon knew. Metatron

had hoped with Jesus Christ's death—the scion being Elyon's nosy eyes and ears—that he might have more time. However, Elyon always did have his sneaky spying ways, some of which Metatron had yet to discover. "Yes, I disobeyed because your orders were unreasonable."

"That wasn't your decision to make. The Eden flock is corrupt. It needs cleansing."

"It's not corrupt. It just doesn't want to be your vassal. And I can't say I blame them. You've done nothing for this planet."

"I gave them life!" God boomed, and Metatron held in a wince as the words reverberated in his skull.

The discomfort didn't stop him from growling, "And now you would punish them for living as they see fit."

Elyon switched subjects. "I banished you so you'd stop causing trouble."

"You banished me because you knew if you tried to order me killed, I'd make sure Heaven saw you for what you really are." And it wasn't the genial God they worshipped.

The next statement was practically spat. "Your mutiny and that of the choir won't go unpunished."

"Really? And how do you plan to mete it? It would require you leaving your precious palace on Heaven. Which we both know won't happen, not with Hell practically on Eden's doorstep."

"I've tolerated much from you, Metatron, but this time, you've gone too far."

"I could say the same. I should have put a stop to your megalomania a millennia ago." Before Elyon got so strong.

"You were weak then, and you are weak now."

"Am I? I dare you to say that to my face." A challenge tossed.

"As you wish," the ominous reply.

The connection severed, and Metatron sighed. There was no turning back now.

Earth was going to war. And Hell might not be its worst threat.

Enjoy the thrilling conclusion in Metatron featuring our favourite archangel and the Templar knight who drives him nuts.